The Lonely

Child

A Novel

GLEN TURNER

Global Publishing House   Los Angeles California

Published by:
Global Publishing House
Compton, California
323-346-2743
Email: mrgturner83@yahoo.com

Distributed by:
Professional Publishing House
1425 W. Manchester Avenue, Ste. B
Los Angeles, California 90047
323-750-3592
Drrosie@aol.com

Cover design by Jay De Vance III
First Printing January 2013
ISBN: 978-0-615-74629-6
Library of Congress Control Number: 2012956277
10987654321

Dedication

*To my son, Glen Turner, Jr, and
to the memory of my mother, Sandra.
Thank you!*

Acknowledgements

I want to acknowledge all my family and friends who instilled me with inspiration, motivation, guidance and help on my journey. I appreciated all of you. You have made a difference in my life.

Table of Contents

Chapter I

~The Custody Battle~

Eugene walked into the Family Court Room with his foster parents, De and Marty, to continue the ongoing custody battle between his biological and foster parents. Born on June 28, 1983, Eugene was brought into this cruel world after several hours of hard labor. The circumstances surrounding him being ushered into existence were told to him by his mother when he was five years old.

While being with no other women, other than his mother, he was now being taken away from her for reasons that were unknown to him at the time. The ongoing custody battle between the biological and foster parents placed Eugene in a compromising place.

The judge later ruled in favor of the foster parents, the Wilsons. The biological parents were accused of child neglect and drug abuse. After several months of an ongoing custody battle and relocating to different foster homes, Eugene Gardner was finally adopted by the Wilsons, and taken into their home to meet and be with his new family. Eugene, being very confused, began his reign of terror by acting out in a rage that was incomprehensible to the Wilsons, who weren't used to such behavior. They tried to do everything within their power to control Eugene. He was a wild one, and he was totally out of control for the rest of the year.

The Wilsons continued to try to work with Eugene, assuming he was just going through a stage from being away from his biological mother. However, as time progressively moved on, Eugene's behavior worsened. It was becoming stressful on the Wilsons, as they had other children to tend to, and Eugene was demanding entirely too much of their attention. Yet, the Wilsons refused to give up on him, especially Mrs. Wilson. Mrs. Wilson repeatedly said, "I see something special in Eugene."

Even though it seemed to be an unbearable task, the Wilsons continued to work with Eugene and managed to get him under control with help from the other children and his biological grandfather (his mother's father).

The Wilsons enrolled Eugene in kindergarten at La Salle Elementary School. Eugene's mother, Sandra, pleaded with the Wilsons to allow her to bring Eugene back home with her. Sandra told the Wilsons, "I want my son, he needs me and I need him. I beg of you. He is all that I have. He gives me the motivation to live and to change."

"What about the drug use?" Mr. Wilson asked.

"I quit," Sandra said. "I'd rather have my son than drugs. I want my son back."

Mrs. Wilson asked, "Will you promise to enroll in a drug program for support?"

"Sure. I will do anything to have Eugene back with me."

After several visits to the mother's home, the Wilsons saw how she had cleaned up her house. She enrolled in an outpatient, drug treatment program, and from all appearances, was now drug-free. They were also worn down by her pleadings, so they agreed to let Eugene go back and live with his mother. He did not get the chance to attend the school they had enrolled him in. Sandra was allowed to take Eugene to live with her in Compton, California. The Wilsons lived in Los Angeles, California, a neighboring city.

The Wilsons wanted to believe that Sandra would change her lifestyle for the child's sake. Periodically, Mrs. Wilson would call to check on them. However, every time she called Eugene would answer the telephone. No matter the time of day or evening, when she would ask to speak to Sandra, he made up excuses as to why his mother could not come to the phone. Eugene would say, "She's sleep," or "She's in the bathroom," or "She will be right back in a few minutes."

Mr. Wilson observed a worried look on his wife's face. He had noticed a change in her demeanor since Eugene was now living with his mother. While spending time alone while the other children were away at school, Mr. Wilson asked Mrs. Wilson, "Honey, what's bothering you?"

"Nothing," she replied.

"I have been with you too many years not to know when something is troublesome to you. What is it, sweetie?"

"I have a feeling that Sandra lied to us. I think she is still hanging out and using drugs. She is never home when I call the house. I have called early mornings, evenings and late nights, but each time I call, Eugene answers the telephone, and he makes up different excuses as to why Sandra can't come to the telephone. I went to her house late one evening, I heard the television, but when I punched the doorbell, the sound from the television diminished. I saw Eugene as he dashed from the living room. I knocked and I called his name several times, but he would not answer. Honey, something is wrong, I just know it."

"Honey, let's just do the right thing for Eugene, and contact the social worker."

As Mrs. Wilson suspected, Sandra had continued to indulge with drugs; she wasn't able to keep her son for long. The Wilson family contacted the social worker, and Eugene was returned to them. This was just the first of several takings, for which Sandra risked her freedom and her life to get her only son back, which, in today's society, would be considered kidnapping.

When Eugene would hear his foster parents talking about Sandra kidnapping him, he would think, *How can someone kidnap their own son? That's real crazy talk?*

This became unbearable for Eugene, and he was too young to know or understand what was really going on. He became depressed and his anger grew out of control. He didn't know who to be angry with—his mom, the Wilsons or the judge who took him away from his mother.

As a child, Eugene picked up on things quickly. Eugene was placed in grade school to learn the basics and to be around other children. Eugene was the second youngest of the three other children at the foster home. Ebony, the youngest, was one year younger than Eugene. Then, there were Niesha and Donte, who were both a year older.

By this time, Eugene had become emotionally and psychologically scarred. His life had taken a downward spiral and he cared less about what others thought or felt about him. Eugene did fairly well in school, until he started first grade in 1988. That's when more behavior problems unfolded for him. The teachers didn't know how to control him and were not willing to deal with a badass kid.

Chapter II

~First Day of School~

Just like any other day, Eugene entered Ms. Thomas's class. Before he could reach his seat, she said, "Eugene, come here!"

Eugene walked to Ms Thomas's desk to see what she wanted. She seemed very unusual to him, but she was his teacher. She told him that she had a referral for him to see the psychologist. He was astounded, as he didn't know who or what she was talking about. She handed him a hall pass and his referral, and said, "Go straight to the principal's office and wait there."

Eugene had no choice but to obey. When he reached the principal's office, the secretary told him, "Have a seat and wait for Mr. Henry to come get you." He waited for about three minutes before Mr. Henry entered the office to get him.

When Mr. Henry saw Eugene, he knew right then and there that he was a trouble child. During the short walk to Mr. Henry's office, which was located in a small room that looked like it used to be a janitor's office, he attempted to make small conversation with Eugene.

"What's your name?" Mr. Henry asked.

"Eugene."

"How old are you, Eugene?"

"I am six years old."

Upon entering the office, Mr. Henry pulled out a chair for Eugene. "Have a seat," he said, and then explained why Eugene was sent to his office. "You were referred to me regarding your behavioral problems and mental state. Do you understand?"

Eugene nodded his head. "Yes."

Mr. Henry then placed photographs on his desk and asked Eugene if he knew what each picture was. Eugene studied the images. The first picture was of grapes, in which Eugene knew. The second picture was a slice of pie, in which Eugene knew this also. The third picture was of a girl smiling while eating ice cream from a cone, in which Eugene also knew this. It became more complicated for Eugene when Mr. Henry asked him what the picture meant to him. For a six year old, that was complicated, because the girl in the picture was doing a variety of things.

Eugene finally replied. "The girl looks like she is happy."

Mr. Henry must have been satisfied with Eugene's answer because he didn't push him any further. He even gave him a lollipop. Just before Mr. Henry allowed him to return to class, he needed to talk to his foster parents. Mr. Henry informed the Wilsons that he would be putting an I.E.P. together on Eugene. They will be monitoring his behavior throughout the rest of the school year. After Mr. Henry finished talking to the Wilsons, Eugene returned back to Ms. Thomas's class.

The school year progressed, but Eugene's behavior did not. It actually worsened. But the school continued to monitor his behavior, with hopes of keeping it in control, helping him to better manage his anger. But, to no avail, eventually, they gave up and decided he would be better off in a special education class. He didn't have a problem with learning. On the contrary, he actually had good grades, but his behavior was unacceptable. He had a bad temper and didn't know how to control his anger.

Instead of the school trying to work with the source of Eugene's frustration and anger, they categorized him as a sociopath. However, they waited until the fourth grade to place him in a special education class, and that did not sit well with Ms. Boyd.

Ms. Boyd was not in favor of Eugene being placed in a special-education class, because she knew a learning disability was not his problem; he was too smart. Knowing it was better for him to be in a regular class, Ms. Boyd had Eugene in her class part-time to help him keep up with what was going on with the rest of the fourth graders versus being in Mr. Bass's special-education class full-time where he wasn't learn anything. She was willing to go that extra mile to help him.

Three years passed, and Eugene finally grew to respect the Wilsons. He realized there was no need to be rebellious toward them any longer, as he was, for the first time, feeling like he was a part of a family. He had a brother and sisters, and a lot of friends.

Things seemed to be getting better for him. He was heavily into sports, which was a way he escaped all his troubles, but little did he know at the time, that meeting people and staying busy kept him content and focused, which kept him from stressing about his mother and father—but mainly his mother.

Chapter III

~Eugene's Mother's Funeral~

It was 1992. Eugene was ten years old, and he continued to go through trials and tribulations that were far too much for a young child to bear, and now he was about to face the worst nightmare ever.

Eugene was in Ms. G's class when he was called to the principal's office. When he reached the principal's office, he saw the Wilsons, and they were dressed up. Eugene was wondering what was going on, because he also saw a look in the Wilsons' eyes that he'd never witnessed before. It was a look of sorrow. They just looked sad to him.

The Wilsons embraced Eugene and said, "We're so sorry."

Eugene looked baffled, as he didn't understand what was taking place. He was thinking, *Grown-ups sure do be acting weird,* and that he was glad he was a kid.

They said to Eugene, "We are taking you to see your mother."

First Eugene was excited because he had not seen his mother in almost five years. But, when they pulled up in the parking lot of a funeral parlor, his excitement turned to confusion and fear. They walked in. The place had a smell to it, but Eugene could not put his finger on what the smell was. A tall, astute man, with his nose in the air, almost uppity-like, man escorted them to a room with an opened casket, and someone lying in it. As Eugene approached the casket, nothing could have prepared him for what he was about to see. Standing in front of the casket, he looked down and quickly stumbled backwards. It was his mother lying there in that casket. He couldn't understand what she was doing there, and why she wasn't moving. Why she wasn't breathing—this was the scariest thing he had ever seen in his young life. Eugene was standing there; he had no clue as to what was going on. His mind was racing a hundred miles per hour.

Finally, Mrs. Wilson wrapped her arms around him and comforted him. She said, "Eugene, your mother is in a better place. She is with God now and she is at peace. Heaven is a peaceful place."

Eugene still didn't understand, but her words eased his pain a little. The Wilsons asked Eugene to stand by his mother's casket, so they could take pictures of him by his mother in the casket. This was strange to Eugene, who rightfully refused to do so. However, the Wilsons were not taking no for an answer. They made Eugene get by the casket to take the pictures. What for? Eugene never knew.

After viewing his mother's body, it was time for the funeral, which was even more dramatic. Eugene's mother was one of five sisters and two brothers. Out of her siblings, she was the first to pass. Actually, she was murdered in cold blood. The Wilsons knew that this would have a big impact on young Eugene's life, so they did all they could to ease the pain. Though, not knowing how this would play out in life in the years to come, they prayed and hoped for the best.

The funeral ceremony was just like any other ghetto funeral. The preacher said things about the deceased that were true and false, because he didn't know the decedent. As the soloist sang, "Precious Lord," the family members began to weep. Eugene started to cry, too. Mrs. Wilson placed her arm around Eugene and wiped his tears with her handkerchief, as she held him tightly in her arms.

She whispered in his ear, "It's okay to cry. Let it out and you will feel better."

The burial was dramatic and sad. When they placed Sandra's body into the walls of the crypt, Eugene knew now that he would never see his mother again, and it hurt him to no end.

After the burial, everyone went to his mother's house and celebrated and mourned, while Eugene and his cousin Jacorie left to go to Bridget's to play arcade games to get his mind off his mother's death. Growing up, Eugene and his Jacorie were tight until they were separated.

Though the years, Eugene was coming to understand his situation and accepted the fact that things were not going to change any time soon. 1992 remained to be a rough year for Eugene. He was going through counseling to help him deal with the mental torment and emotional developments, so that he could get over the death of his mother.

Even though Eugene did not live with his mother he loved her and knew that she loved him, and it was his hope that one day he and his mother would reunite. Sandra's death created a void and an empty feeling in Eugene's life. Eugene knew, without a doubt, that the Wilsons loved him and he was a part of the family.

Eugene's world changed drastically. He began to really act out after the death of his mother. His acting out was the only way he knew to express how he was feeling, while suppressing his true inner feelings. Truthfully, he was was grieving the loss of his mother. Although she hadn't been the ideal mother, he loved her and missed her just the same.

Chapter IV

~Irrational Behavior~

One day, while attending school, Eugene was walking the school yard with his friend James—who lived next door to Eugene—and they were talking about their basketball game. They both played for the park. While having this conversation with his friend, Eugene saw a girl by the name of Courtney, who he liked, but he didn't know if she liked him. He never bothered to ask her to find out.

Eugene was being mean to Courtney because he didn't know any other way to treat her. When they made eye contact, Eugene hurried off to start chasing Courtney around the playground. He found half of an orange. He picked it up and threw it at Courtney, and the half-nasty orange hit Courtney in the head and stuck there for a minute. Eugene, James and others, who had witnessed this episode, laughed. Courtney's feelings were shattered that day, and it was all because Eugene had taken his feelings out on someone who hadn't done anything to him.

Courtney was not the first to feel Eugene's rage of terror. This was the start of a troubled child acting out in a manor incomprehensible to those who hadn't experienced an upsetting and emotionally disturbed childhood.

1993, Eugene is eleven years old, in the sixth grade, and still attending LaSalle Elementary School. Eugene was improving slowly. At school, two teachers—Ms. P and Ms. G.—stood up and fought for him. Ms. G was Eugene's fifth-grade teacher, who also believed that Eugene was a good kid, even though he was the cause of Ms. G having high blood pressure. She still cared about him and wanted to see him progress while at La Salle Elementary School. 1993 was the last year of elementary for Eugene. That was the year of graduation, if all was to go well for him.

At home with the Wilsons, Eugene now considered the Wilson's his parents. He was even calling Mrs. Wilson mother. Yes, things were improving. However, Eugene was still dealing with behavioral problems. The psychologist put Eugene on medication called Melaril, which would supposedly calm him down. The medication did not help; it only made Eugene drowsy, which made it difficult for him to focus on his schoolwork. It didn't take long for the Wilsons to see that the medication given to Eugene was affecting not only his physical, but his mental state also.

One morning, Mrs. Wilson gave Eugene his medication, but she didn't give him the prescribed amount. Instead, she gave him more than usual, and she made him drink the medicine straight. Melaril is a liquid medication that is mixed with water, and measured to ensure the right dosage is taken. However, Mrs. Wilson felt that the normal amount wasn't enough, so she increased the amount of medicine, which sent Eugene into a state of lethargy whereby he couldn't focus on anything. He couldn't eat anything. Eugene felt that way for about two days. When that happened, Mrs. Wilson didn't know what to do. She was thinking that Eugene might not make it, but he did. When he did make it, Mrs. Wilson decided that she would no longer give Eugene the medication.

For the remainder of the school year, things were going kind of smoothly, until Eugene went into a rage and had an altercation with another student who he kept punching him repeatedly for no apparent reason. When the teacher, Ms. P, broke up the fight, she asked, "Eugene what happened?"

Eugene was being defiant. He said, "It's none of your business, so stay out of it."

Ms. P took a jump rope and whipped him in front of the whole class. Eugene fought back the tears as his pride was put on display in front of everyone. After more than a few strikes, Ms. P gave up on the whipping. However, that was just the beginning for the students of La Salle Elementary School, as many more felt the terror of Eugene's troubled childhood.

Thursday, one week later, while sitting in Ms. G's class, Eugene was joking with a girl who sat next to him. For no reason, he called her a bitch. The girl was rightfully offended, not understanding why Eugene would call her such a name, but he wasn't going to get away with it. With the cast she wore on her broken arm, she hit him on the side of his face. Eugene picked up a chair and threw at the girl, but luckily, she quickly moved out of the way. However, it wasn't so lucky for Eugene nor Ms. G, as the chair landed at her feet. Ms. G was beyond angry, as she went into a frenzy rage, screaming, "Eugene! What's wrong with you? Have you lost your mind?"

Ms. G said to her class, "I want you to remain calm and to behave and be quite while I escort Eugene to the principal's office." She took Eugene by his arm out of the room and to the principal's office. She explained to the principal what had taken place in the classroom.

The principal turned to Eugene and asked, "Eugene, would you please tell me what happened?

"You ain't gonna believe what I say anyway, so why should I bother to tell you anything?"

"I really want to hear your side of the story and I have no reason not to believe you. So, let's hear it."

Ms. G said to the principal, "I am leaving now. I left my classroom unattended." She turned to Eugene and said, "Eugene, I still see greatness in you."

The principal said to Ms. G., "I will deal with him on this matter." The principal recognized that Eugene was emotionally disturbed and was a very angry young man who could not control his impulses. He understood Eugene; however, he knew that he had to do something about his behavior in the classroom. Eugene was suspended from school for three days.

Chapter V

~The School Trip~

On Eugene's return to school on Wednesday morning, everyone seemed to be so excited about something. Eugene asked his boy, James, "What's happening?"

He replied, "Everybody is happy about the field trip to San Francisco next week."

Eugene just knew he would not be able to go. Even though he was doing well in his schoolwork, his behavior had not improved. He knew Mrs. Wilson was not going to pay for him to go. He just went on about his business the whole day.

In a P.T.A. meeting, the teachers, and some volunteers were discussing the trip, talking about some of the students, in which Eugene was one of them. They concluded that Eugene should be allowed to go on the trip. Despite his behavior, they felt he was improving. Two of them decided they would contribute money to pay for Eugene to go on the three-day trip, which was the following week. They called Mrs. Wilson and told her what they wanted to do and asked if it was okay with her, in which she said it was fine. They asked her not to mention anything to Eugene until it was time for him to go on the trip. She agreed. Then the telephone line went dead.

Everybody went along through the week like any normal week, but all was looking towards the following week, everybody except Eugene. One day, before the trip, Eugene went to school and did his work as usual, then went on about his business during the day. The day seemed to drag on, but finally, it was over, and it was time for Eugene to go home. When he got home, he parted from his friends and went into the house. Mrs. Wilson was waiting on him to see how his day went. They made small talk then Eugene went to his room.

The day of the trip...

Eugene was awakened that morning by Mrs. Wilson. He asked, "What's going on?" He knew he didn't have school because all the sixth graders were going on a trip.

Mrs. Wilson just smiled for a minute. Then she spoke, choosing her words carefully. "Eugene, sweetie, you are going on that trip, too."

Eugene said, "For real?" He couldn't believe what he was hearing, but he knew Mrs. Wilson was serious. He said, "Thank you."

Mrs. Wilson replied, "Don't thank me. Thank your teachers." And with that, she said, "Get dressed. You don't want to miss that bus."

They had a good time in San Francisco, especially Eugene. He came back so excited, until he almost couldn't control himself. As the bus pulled in front of the school, Eugene walked to his teachers and hugged them and thanked them for allowing him to go on the trip. Eugene made it through school. He even attended his sixth-grade graduation, which was held in the auditorium of LA Southwest Community College. The graduation was off the hook. The last year of elementary school was a good year for Eugene. Everyone said their good-byes. Some knew they would never see each other again and for some, they would. However, they all would experience a dramatic change in their lives, especially Eugene.

Chapter VI

~Affiliated~

It was the first day of school, and Eugene was excited about attending Horace Mann Middle School because he had heard so much about it. After getting dressed and putting on his best cologne, and he was off to school. But first, he stopped next door to see if James was ready for school, so they could walk to school together. Then they were off.

As they entered the front entrance of the school, the atmosphere seemed different from elementary school. No matter how much they thought they were prepared; nothing could prepare them for what they were in store for.

They had to go to their homeroom class, which they had the same homeroom teacher, Ms. Johnson. In middle school, Eugene had six classes. First period was Math, which was also his homeroom class. Second period was computer class, then Nutrition. Third period was English. Fourth period was Science, then lunch. Fifth period was History, and sixth period was P.E.

Eugene enjoyed his first day of school. He got to meet new people, especially Wacky who later would introduce Eugene to gangs, and that's when Eugene really goes through a dramatic change.

Eugene would later become affiliated with one of the organizations in America that has been criticized and ridiculed for their known reputation. This is what the government calls today, in-land terrorists. Eugene and Wacky shared the same P.E. class. Wacky was a year older than Eugene. For the remainder of the first semester, Eugene spent most of his time meeting people and getting to know them.

Eugene met Keyonna, and she became his first girl friend while attending Horace Mann. Keyonna was sweet and pretty. She had beautiful smooth brown skin and pretty brown eyes. Eugene was really digging Keyonna. They both shared History class together. Their teacher's name was Mrs. Baker. She was one of the best teachers at Horace Mann. She cared about her students and was willing to help them. Eugene enjoyed Mrs. Baker's class. Eugene and Keyonna had a cool relationship going on, but there was only one problem. Keyonna's father didn't approve of her having a boyfriend, especially after meeting Eugene. He disapproved of Eugene. Eugene was now gang banging, and that didn't make matters any better. That was the reason Keyonna's father didn't approve of Eugene. But his daughter favored thug niggers.

Eugene was from a known street gang called 2DCG. He went by the nickname, Lil' Loc. Eugene and several of his homeboys were attending school together, and they were really acting like fools. Eugene's brother was also attending the same school, and they both were affiliated with gangs.

One Tuesday, while in Nutrition, Eugene and his homeboys were sitting at a table, just talking and joking around when five other males from a rival gang approached the table. They said to Eugene, "Fuck two dirty children."

Eugene reacted by hitting one of them in his mouth, then the remainder of the males from both gangs started to rumble. The school police came, and everybody ran except for Lil' Loc (Eugene), who continued to beat on the rival gang member, who was unconscious. If it were not for the school police, Lil' Loc would have killed the boy.

After the smoke cleared, Lil' Loc was in the school office waiting to see what they would do with him.

Officer Tate called Eugene into the office, and motioned toward an empty chair. "Have a seat," he said, taking a seat behind his desk. When Eugene sat, Officer Tate clasped his hands and peered at Eugene with contempt. "I know about you," he began. "Your name has been ringing around the school for a long time. I also know that you did not start that fight, so I'm going to give you a pass, but you will be suspended for three days and the incident will be documented. Do you have anything to say?"

Eugene leaned forward, resting his elbows on his knees. "Naw," he said in a disrespectful manger.

Officer Tate sighed, disgusted with the young boys who had nothing better to do with their lives besides gang-bang, but he also sensed that Eugene was a good kid with a bad attitude and steered in the wrong direction.

Officer Tate wrote Eugene's name on a white card the police used to identify gang members, with their nickname(s) and the gang their gang affiliations.

Eugene was sent home, and when he made it home, Mrs. Wilson was waiting for him in the living room. As he came through the door, Mrs. Wilson was all over him with a track from his Hot Wheels set, whipping him. Mrs. Wilson was swinging wildly with the track, and Eugene was trying to block the track from hitting him in the face, which seemed to have made matters worsen, as she started calling Eugene all types of names while whipping him. When she finally calmed down, she said, "Eugene, go to your room and I will deal with you later."

Mrs. Wilson called Eugene to the kitchen for dinner. Everybody else was already sitting at the table when Eugene walked into the kitchen. At first, Eugene thought that Mrs. Wilson was going to send him back to his room because he was on punishment, but she told him, "Eugene, sit at the table with the rest of the family. And after you are done eating, you are to wash the dishes and clean the kitchen."

Eugene responded, "WHAT?"

Mrs. Wilson replied, "Look Eugene, I don't want to hear nothing from you and this is just the beginning for you. I am going to teach you about getting suspended from school."

This was just the beginning of many times Eugene would be put to labor doing house chores by himself. This continued on for the seventy-two hours Eugene was suspended from school. He wasn't allowed to go outside with his friends, and every morning and night, he had to do thorough cleaning because Mrs. Wilson wasn't going for a half ass-cleaning job. She made him scrub the bathroom, kitchen walls and more.

The following week...Monday

Eugene, his brother Donte, James and Kevin met up, so they could walk to school together

James said, "Eugene, man you are the talk of the school."

Eugene asked, "Is that right?"

Kevin interrupted and said, "Hey, my nigga...niggas and bitches are talking about you are crazy and how you damn near killed that fool Steve. Plus, my nigga, the bitches are talking about you are cute and shit."

Eugene started to laugh. "Damn, I'm like a ghetto celebrity," he said, as he laughed again.

Donte said, "Yeah, all that's cool, but you know them bitch-ass niggas might try to catch you slipping."

Eugene replied, "Damn, bro, you are right, but fuck those fools. If they try anything, I'll be ready and best believe that."

They all gave each other dap and said, "And we will all be ready." That's the kind of love they had for each other.

As they reached the school, people were trying to holler at Eugene. As they approached the front entrance, more homies were waiting for him. There was the homie Wacky and Lil' Wacky, Lil' Pest and Puppet, Scrappy and Devil Loc. Everyone said their greetings and then departed to their classes.

As Eugene walked to his class, Lisa and Thea from one of his classes approached him and asked, "Can we walk with you?"

Eugene replied, "I don't care."

They started talking about how they heard about how he whipped on Steve and how the homies had a rumble with them RBP niggas that same day. Unbeknownst to Eugene, Lisa and Thea were trying to play both sides of the fences. And this could be trouble for Eugene if he's not careful.

As they reached their class, Lisa and Thea gave Eugene their phone numbers. Lisa whispered in Eugene's ear, "I like you."

Eugene went through the day without any problems. After school, Eugene and his homeboys went to the burger stand where they sometimes hung out.

At Steve's house…

Lisa and Thea walked to the front door of Steve's house. They rang the doorbell. As they were let into the house, they saw about twelve other niggas sitting around the living room, holding weapons from baseball bats to sticks and knives.

Steve, who was still trying to recuperate from his injuries, asked Lisa, "What do you have for me?"

She then replied, "Lil' Loc and his homies are at the burger stand right now."

Steve asked, "How many of them are there?

Lisa replied, "It's about ten of them."

Steve asked, "Do you know who else besides Lil' Loc?'

Steve's homies were saying, "Fuck all them bitch-ass niggas. Let's go serve them niggas. Homie, what are we waiting on?"

Steve paid them no mind. But, he said to them, "We are going to serve them. I just want to know who is all up there."

Lisa said, "It's Devil Loc, Locsta, Pest, Wacky and Lil' Wacky, Scrappy, Puppet, Demon and Lil' Pest."

"Damn, they are going to be heated," Steve said.

When Steve's homies heard this, they started saying, "Man, we don't have any heat and we ain't trying to get shot."

Steve said, "Shut the fuck up, ain't nobody going to get shot today, at least not none of us. We just have to rethink this, but I'm going to get that nigga Lil' Loc. I can't let that shit he did to me ride."

Steve looked around at his homies, and said, "I am going to holler at you another day."

Everyone left Steve's house except Lisa and Thea. Steve and Lisa went into his room, which is located in the back of the house, to talk in private. When they get into the room, Steve said to Lisa, "I want you to try and find out where Lil' Loc lives."

"For what? What are you trying to do?"

"I ain't trying to do nothing. I just want to know where Lil' Loc lives." Then, he asked, Lisa, "Do you love me?"

"Yes!

"Lisa, do you trust me?"

" Sure, I trust you."

Thea called out for Lisa. "I am ready to go home," she said.

"Damn, I can't stand that bitch," said Steve. "Why do you be fucking with her?"

"She's my best friend."

Steve let it go and told Lisa, "I will holler at you later."

Lisa and Thea left.

On the way home…

As Lisa and Thea were walking home together, they made small talk about school and other stuff. Thea asked Lisa, "What did you and Steve talk about when you were in the room?"

"Nothing."

But Thea didn't buy it, so she kept on pushing the issue. "Girl, why are you bullshitting? Y'all were in the room for about twenty minutes, and y'all weren't fucking because I didn't hear any moaning," said Thea.

"Damn, you sure are a nosey bitch, aren't you?"

"That's me, so when we get to my house, come in and tell me everything. You know you want to anyway."

When they reached Thea's house, they went straight to Thea's room. As they sat down, Thea asked, "What did he say?"

"He was asking me if I knew where Lil' Loc lived."

"What did you tell him?"

"I told him I didn't know where Lil' Loc lived."

"So you lied to him? Girl, you must be feeling Lil'; Loc."

"Yeah, I think I am. Plus I'm getting tired of Steve."

"Well, if the truth be told, I'm not mad at you, because that nigga Lil' Loc is something else, with his fine self." Both girls laughed.

Lisa said, "Damn girl, I know he's fine. He just doesn't know what he does to me."

"Girl, you better stop before you end up having an orgasm all over my bed and my momma just washed this comforter." Both girls laughed again. "Lisa, now on the serious side, girl, what are you going to do?"

"I don't know, but I have better figure something out because if Steve keeps trying to fuck with Lil' Loc, he's going to end up getting killed. I wouldn't want that to happen no matter how stupid that boy Steve act."

"Yeah, I feel you, girl, because Lil' Loc and his squad is not playing."

"You would think that Steve would have learned his lesson by now, especially after what Lil' Loc did to him the first time."

"Shit, he was on the verge of dying then if it wasn't for the school police."

"Yeah, but look, girl, I'm about to go home. I'll talk to you later, okay?"

"Yeah, okay."

Lisa and Thea lived around the corner from each other.

Chapter VII

~The Come Up~

Back at the burger stand...
Eugene and his homies were about to leave the burger stand and go to Wacky's house. They were going to smoke some marijuana and check on a shipment of guns that were supposed to come. Their homeboys, Spooks and Looney, are supposed to go get the shipment and meet the rest of the homies at Wacky's house. While waiting, they were smoking marijuana, passing blunts around in a circle and talking about how it was going to go down when they got the shipment. The guns they had before were seized in a raid, so they had to start all over again.

Locsta spoke up and said, "Check it out! I got this cool spot that we can set up shop in, but first we need some cash flow."

Lil' Loc responded, "We have spent all our money on the guns."

Locsta replied, "Don't trip, I got an establishment that we can run up in and hit for a cool little something to get on our feet. Who's with that?"

"I got you on the line up already, so don't trip," said Lil' Loc.

Wacky said, "Add me to the list, my nigga."

"For sho', you're on there," said Locsta.

"Add me too, my nigga," said Devil Loc. "I'm in."

Locsta started explaining the hit. "The lick is like this; you have one security guard that sits at the door. Devil Loc, you gon' go through the door last. As soon as you come through the door, you book the guard.

"Wacky, you are driving. Lil' Loc and I are going to lay the two employees and the manager down.

"Demon, you get the money from the register and get all the jewelry. I'm going to take the manager to the back to make him open the safe. Then we're going to tie all of them up, while Lil' Loc and Devil Loc stay with their guns drawn down on them. This way, they won't get any crazy ideas. Then, we are out of there. If everybody sticks to the script, everything will go smoothly."

A car drives up with music cranked up loud. Wacky said, "That's Spooks and Looney."

Locsta said, "Tell them niggas to come on in."

As Spooks and Looney entered the house, they were carrying two crates. As they set the crates down on the table, Looney rushed back outside to the car to get a longer crate.

"Somebody get a crowbar, so we can pop these crates open," said Spooks.

Lil' Loc handed Spook a crowbar. "Here, my nigga."

They all gathered around as Spooks popped one of the smaller crates open. When they saw what was inside, they all said, "DAMN!!!" There were several types of guns in the small crate—9mm; Berettas; 40 Glocks; 45 Smith & Westerns; 380 Berettas; A.R. 15's; AK 47's, and SK German K's. They all started to celebrate for their achievement and they had plenty of ammunition.

"My niggas, Thursday morning it's going down," said Locsta. "So, Lil' Loc, Demon, Devil Loc and Wacky, be ready."

Spooks asked," What are you talking about?"

Locsta replied, "We are about to hit this lick that's going to really put us in the game."

Looney said, "Shit, what's cracking? How can I be down?"

Locsta replied, "The roster is full, but don't trip."

"For sho', it's cool. I'll catch y'all on the next one, plus we all together anyway, so be safe and do the damn thing."

Everybody said, "For sho'."

Shorty Loc stated, I'm about to go to the house and see what's cracking."

Lil' Loc said, "All right, my nigga; we'll holler at you. I'm about to do some moving myself."

They all started to depart, but first they grabbed their guns.

At home…

Eugene got home and went straight to his room. He put the two 9mms in his stashing spot that he and his brother Donte made underneath their bunk beds. Just as he finished putting the guns away, Mrs. Wilson called for him to come downstairs to her bedroom. As Eugene went to her room to see what she wanted, he was thinking about the lick that his homie Locsta had put them up on. Eugene was so zoned out that he didn't hear her.

Mrs. Wilson yelled, "BOY! Did you hear me?"

"Oh excuse me, Ma, I didn't hear you. What did you say?"

"Boy, you better stop sleepwalking and pay attention. I said, 'How was your day?'"

"My day was all right. We saw a movie called the *Outsiders* today at school in Mr. Smith's class and we have to do a report about it. Other than that, my day was cool. What about your day?"

"I just did a little cleaning up and I watched my stories." Their conversation was interrupted by the phone ringing, and Eugene used it as an excuse to escape back to his room. Mrs. Wilson answered the phone. "Hello!"

The caller on the other end replied, "It's Locsta. Is Eugene home, Mrs. Wilson?"

Mrs. Wilson responded, "This is who?"

"It's Donald Locsta."

Mrs. Wilson yelled, "Eugene, telephone and for you. You can get the phone in the living room. Eugene goes to the living room to get the phone. "Okay, Ma, I got it."

Mrs. Wilson hung up the telephone and went about doing her chores as usual. Eugene picked up the phone and looked around before speaking. "What's happening, my nigga?"

"Nothing much, my nigga, just in the house chilling. So what's cracking with you? Are you ready?"

"Yeah, I was born ready."

"Now that's what I'm talking about, my nigga. That's why I already had you in the start-up line."

"For sho', my nigga. You know what's happening with me. Plus school is about to be over and this is the year for some of us, you feel me?"

"Yeah, I feel you and we are going to be all the way right, so don't trip."

"I was just hollering. Did you holler at that bitch Lisa yet? You know that bitch be on you."

"Is that right? I be hollering every now and then, but I be on turf business."

"I feel that, but holler at her. You know her best friend Thea?"

"Yeah. What about her?"

"Well, nigga, I'm hollering at her. She's thicker than a Snickers and she's pretty."

"My nigga you better try to hit that," said Eugene.

"Don't worry about me, I'm going to take her down, you just get with Lisa."

"I'm on that, my nigga, one-love…I'm out," said Eugene.

Eugene decided to call Lisa. He got his phone book and found Lisa's phone number.

At Lisa's house…
The phone rung. "Hello."

"Is this Lisa?"

"Yes. This is she. Who is this?"

"This is Lil' Loc, Lisa."

"Oh, how're you doing?"

"I'm doing better now that I'm talking to you."

Lisa laughed, "Boy, you're crazy."

"What, crazy about getting with you?"

"What did you say?" Lisa replied still laughing.

"You heard me, don't act like you didn't."

"I was just making sure that I heard you correct, but ain't you fucking with Keyonna?"

"Yeah, but she ain't acting right and plus I'm trying to find someone to take the number one position."

"Well, you might be talking to her now."

"See that's what I'm talking about, claim prize and be about it."

"I am about it and that you will see."

"Is that a threat?"

"Yeah, but in a good way." They both laughed.

"Girl, you are crazy."

"You are correct. Like you said, I'm crazy about you."

"Well, since it's like that then let's make it official. It's you and me."

"Yeah, it's you and me, baby. Goodbye, Eugene."

"Okay, talk to you later."

Wednesday night...

Locsta, Little Loc, Devil Loc, Wacky and Demon are all at Wacky's house preparing for the lick they would hit in the morning.

Locsta said, "Wacky already got the G-ride, we get the heaters, we don't need no masks because the jewelry store don't have any cameras. Everybody knows what they are supposed to do. There is no room for mistakes."

Devil Loc said, "If the security guard tries anything slick, I'm gonna smoke his ass." They all laughed.

Little Loc replied, "My nigga, I don't think he's going to try anything once he sees the barrel of that 45."

Locsta, on a serious note, said. "The guard ain't going to try shit, so calm your trigger-happy ass down."

"I was just saying. If he try anything, pistol whoop him, but we ain't trying to kill nobody. Like I said, stick to the script and everything will go smoothly."

Demon asked, "So we meet here in the morning, right?"

"Yeah, we meet here at Wacky's house. From here we go take care of business, so everybody be here by 8:35 a.m. Okay, let's move."

Locsta and Lil' Loc were going in the same direction.

Locsta asked, "So what's happening, my nigga?"

"Ain't much, just ready to do this."

"That's right, and what's cracking with Lisa, did you do that?"

Lil' Loc replied, "Yeah, my nigga, I did that and she said she's with it and that she wants to be my girl. "

"That's right, so she's your girl now! I'm going to holler; see you in the morning, one-love."

"One-love, my nigga!" Eugene said.

Chapter VIII

~The Robbery~

Thursday morning…

Eugene was awake at 6:00 a.m. He and Donte both were awake.

"Are you ready?" Donte asked.

Eugene responded, "Yeah, I'm ready. I'm a little nervous, but I'll be all right."

"Be safe and I got you covered with Ma."

"Thanks, man. You know I got you once this is over with."

Eugene dressed in a black and gray plaid shirt, black Docker pants and black hush puppies, with both 9mms on his waistline. It took him twenty minutes to eat, get dressed and leave. He was off to Demon's house to pick him up. It took him about ten minutes to walk to Demon's house.

As Eugene reached Demon's house, he was thinking about what was about to go down. He knocked on Demon's bedroom window. Demon was awakened from the knocking sound on his window. He got up and went to the window and looked out to see his boy, Lil' Loc, there. He smiled, lifted the window and said, "Come to the back door."

Lil' Loc went to the back door and Demon opened the door for him. Little Loc said, "What's cracking, my nigga?"

"Shit, just getting up."

"Damn, I can tell because you still got morning breath."

"Fuck you, nigga, come on let's go to my room before my granny wakes up."

"So are you ready?"

Demon tried to answer with a toothbrush and toothpaste in his mouth. "Yeah I'm ready."

Lil' Loc said, "My nigga, get yourself together so we can go."

It took Demon about forty-five minutes to get ready, which wasn't too much of a problem because he lived five minutes from Locsta who was to give them a ride to Wacky's house to meet up with Devil-Loc and Wacky.

On the way to Locsta's house, Little Loc and Demon sparked up a blunt to calm their nerves. They reached Locsta's house about five minutes later. Lil' Loc knocked on the door and Locsta answered the door to let them in.

"What's cracking, my niggas?" Locsta asked.

Lil' Loc responded, "Ain't nothing much, ready to handle this business."

Demon said, "Yeah, ready to handle business."

"Right, right, that's what we going to do, just give me a minute then we can move," said Locsta.

Twenty minutes later, Locsta, Lil' Loc and Demon left Locsta's house to go to Wacky's house to meet up with Wacky and Devil Loc.

⟨⟨⟩⟩

Wacky's house...

As they reached Wacky's house, Wacky and Devil Loc was sitting on the porch. They pulled up to the house and Locsta stopped the car so that they could get out. As they walked up to the house, they exchanged greetings and each individual was given a pair of Blockers sunglasses, and a fitted baseball hat. Everyone was ready to go. Wacky went to get the g-ride, which was a Ford Explorer. They then headed to complete their mission.

The lick...

They drove to the jewelry store to rob it. Wacky dropped Locsta, Lil' Loc, Devil Loc and Demon off and parked up the street. The jewelry store was just opening, so they weren't aware of the four young black males coming their way. Locsta and Lil' Loc went in first, then Demon. As soon as Devil Loc came through the door, he drew down on the guard who was about to get up because now he thought something was up, but he was too late. With the guard booked, Locsta and Lil' Loc drew down on the two employees and the manager.

 Locsta yelled, "Get the fuck down! This is a robbery, so don't nobody say shit."

Immediately, Demon went to strip the cash register and open the jewelry cases to get the jewelry.

Locsta yelled, "Stay faced down." He said to the manager, "Come with me." He then asked, "Where's the safe? And don't play any games."

The manager said, "It's over here. You can have whatever you want. Please don't hurt me."

Locsta smacked the manager upside his head. "Didn't I say don't say shit?" Open the motherfucking safe!" The manager opened the safe. "Put everything in the bag and make it quick. Where's the tape?"

Lil' Loc said, "Right here."

"Tie them up and let's get out of here."

Back at Wacky's house…

Wacky dumped the g-ride with Locsta following him in his car. They returned and started to count the money and check out the jewelry. When it was all said and done, they had an estimated $289,000.00 cash and about $400,000.00 in jewelry. For them, that was a lot, and they were stupid balling. For the remainder of the year, they played it cool. They ended up setting up shop and doing their thing. They tried to remain low-key.

Lil' Loc and Lisa became tighter and they were officially a hot couple. Lil' Loc and Keyonna broke up behind Lisa, but Lil'

Loc didn't trip. Word got back to Steve, who was furious when he heard about Lil' Loc and Lisa.

Steve remarked, "Who that nigga think he is? He fucked me up and now he's fucking with my bitch? And she is his girl? Man, fuck him and that bitch, he's going to get his!"

New Year's Eve…

Little Loc, Locsta, Devil Loc, Ant Dogg, Demon and Wacky threw a New Year's Eve party at the Embassy Suites, and everybody was there. Lisa and Thea were there with some of their friends. It was a New Year's to remember. Everyone had a ball. On the count down for the New Year, Lil' Loc and Locsta was at the table with Lisa and Thea talking. The countdown began: 10, 9, 8, 7, 6, 5, 4, 3, 2, 1…Happy New Year!!! They all kissed and told each other, "I love you!" Lil' Loc and Locsta looked at each other and said, "Damn, what a year!"

Chapter IX

~Retaliation~

Ninth Grade…

The start of the ninth grade for Eugene was very exciting because he was ready for it. He had his gear ready, and he still had money from the robbery. He was just being careful on how he spent his money. He had big plans for the future. Eugene had plans of buying a car just as soon as he turned fifteen, so he spent his money wisely. He was also selling weed at the spot that he and his homie had acquired.

Mrs. Wilson started getting suspicious of Eugene. He was giving her money to put up for him, and he didn't have a job. She figured something was going on, but she didn't say anything just as long as Eugene didn't bring any problems to the house or get caught for any crimes. It was hard for her to deal with all the kids she had, so the money came in handy.

Eugene prepared himself for school. He had his outfit out and ready to go—light blue Guess jeans, a number 8 Troy Aikman Dallas Cowboys jersey, with a Pro-Club t-shirt and his patent leather Jordan's. He also wore his gold link chain. He was geared up. Eugene looked himself over in the mirror and loved the way he looked. Now, it was time to go to school, but before leaving, Eugene grabbed his backpack and his 380 Berretta. Now, he was off.

On the way to school, he stopped next door to get James so they could go to school together. This year they were taking the bus to school. Eugene knocked at James' door. James mother asked, "Who is it?"

"It's me, Mrs. Johnson, Eugene!"

Mrs. Johnson opened the door. "Come on in, boy. James is in his room getting ready. You are looking sharp and handsome."

"Thank you, Mrs. Johnson."

Eugene walked past Mrs. Johnson toward James' room. When he entered, James was getting dressed.

"What's up, nigga?

"Nothing. I'm just trying to get ready for school."

"I'm going to play Madden while you finish getting ready for school."

"Go ahead, you need to work on your game, and by the way, where did you get that gold link?"

"I bought it from one of the homies, and what do you mean by I need to work on my game? I can beat you anytime and any place."

"Yeah right, nigga."

"You know I'm right, nigga, stop stalling and get dressed so we can get to school and clown."

"It's going down this year, my nigga."

"Yeah, for sho', are you ready?"

"Yeah, we can go now. You sure are in a hurry to get to school, what's happening?"

"Nothing. I just want to get there. It's the start of the first semester of the ninth grade."

"I feel you, let's go."

"Hold on, I want to show you something. Shut the door."

James closed his door and asked, "What is it?"

"Check it out!" He pulled the gun out of his backpack and showed it to James.

"What kind of gun is that, and where did you get it?"

"It's a 380 Berretta and I got it from the homie Looney."

They walked to the bus stop and waited for the bus to come so they could head to school. As they got off the bus in front of the burger stand, which was a block away from the school, there was a crowd of kids hanging around.

Eugene said, "See, my nigga, I told you it was going to be live."

"Yeah, it's live."

Eugene heard someone calling his name. "Lil' Loc, Lil' Loc." When he saw it was Lisa, he said, "What's up, boo?"

Lisa said, "I missed you, Lil' Loc."

"I missed you, too."

James said, "Oh how sweet!"

Lisa asked Eugene, "How was your vacation?"

"It was straight and I didn't do too much. I just fucked with the homies and had some fun. What about you, how was your trip to Denver?"

"My vacation was off the hook. I went to see my Aunt Karen, and kicked it with all my cousins, who are just dying to meet you because I told them so much about you."

"Is that right, like what?"

"I told them how you represent me and how we are so much in love. I even showed them the picture of you and me at the pier."

"Okay, it's cool."

Eugene turned to James and said, "Let's get to school before we are late. James, is you ready?"

"Yeah, Eugene..."

"Well, let's go before we get caught in the tardy sweep. You know how they be tripping." They barely made it to school in time, but they made it.

That day seemed to drag on and Eugene couldn't wait for school to end, so he could hit the block. Eugene's patience was wearing out. He was about tired of school, so his attention span was short. So he started to act out in class by disrupting other students who were trying to learn. When the bell did sound for school to end, Eugene rushed out of class. As he walked to the exit, James, Lisa and Thea were waiting for him. Eugene put his arm around Lisa and kissed her as he asked her, "What's up, boo?"

Lisa replied, "Nothing. I was wondering if you were going to walk me home."

Eugene agreed to walk Lisa home. Suddenly a car horn blew, and Eugene turned around to look. He saw Locsta in a pearl white Cutlass on gold d's. Eugene, Lisa, Thea and James stopped walking as the car pulled up to the curb. Locsta rolled down the window and called for Lil' Loc.

"What's up, my nigga?" Lil' Lock said.

Locsta said, "Ain't too much, is that Lisa, Thea and James?"

"Yeah."

Locsta said, "Hi, Lisa. Thea, come here."

Thea walked to the passenger side of the car, opened the door and got in. Locsta then said, "My nigga, Lil' Loc, you straight, y'all want a ride?"

Lil' Loc looked at Lisa and James, and then he said, "No, we cool, but I'll catch up with you later."

"All right, my nigga, holler back."

Lil' Loc replied, "Yeah, my nigga."

Lil' Loc, Lisa and James continued to walk on. As they walked up the street, a car sped by them.

Lil' Loc asked, "Damn, James did you see that?"

"Yeah, my nigga. I saw that; them fools are driving crazy. Do you know them?"

"Hell, no I don't know them fools, but I know they better be careful before they fuck around and get busted."

"Them niggas is crazy, for real," said James.

"Yeah, whatever. Like I said, them fools better be careful."

Lisa knew the guys in the car were Steve and a few of his boys. Things had quieted down around the neighborhood for the past weeks, so Lisa didn't want to startle Lil' Loc about her knowing who the guys were in the car. Lisa never told Lil' Loc that she and Steve used to be a couple because she didn't know how he would react, and she was afraid. She was just waiting for the right time to tell Lil' Loc.

She wasn't afraid of Lil' Loc but she was afraid of the relationship taking a dramatic change. She didn't want to lose Lil' Loc. Finally, they were almost to Lisa's house. James continued to walk on as Eugene and Lisa made a right turn in the direction of Lisa's house.

Eugene said, "All right, my nigga, I'll catch up with you."

James said, "For sho' homie, see you later. Be careful."

"You know me, homie."

"Yeah, that's what I'm talking about, and Lisa keep the homie out of trouble. I'm gone."

"Bye, James," Lisa responded, waving goodbye.

Lisa and Eugene continued to walk until they reached Lisa's front door. Lisa rumbled through her purse to get her keys. Eugene just stood on the porch waiting.

Eugene said, "Damn, girl, you can't find your keys or what?"

"They are in here, just calm down. Okay, I found them."

As she unlocked the door and they walked in the house, the phone started ringing. The phone rang about five times before she answered.

"Hello," Lisa answered.

The caller responded, "What's cracking with you, baby girl?"

"Who is this?" Lisa asked.

"You act like you don't know anybody no more since you fucking with that buster ass nigga, Lil' Loc. Don't play dumb, bitch."

Lisa said, "Fuck you," and she hang up the phone.

"What's cracking, why you looking mad and shit?" Eugene asked.

"Nothing. It's nothing!

On the other side of the town...

Steve was sitting in his room laughing and enjoying the prank call he just played on Lisa. He was going to teach her a lesson for back stabbing him. He couldn't believe she would do that to him. Sleeping with the enemy was the utmost betrayal. But fuck it. Steve was sure they both would get what was coming to them. For right now, he was just going to continue to remain low key until he could put his plan into effect.

Back at Lisa's house...

Lisa and Eugene sat on the couch watching *Menace II Society* on the big screen TV. Lisa rested her head on Eugene's shoulder and said, "I love you."

"I love you, too."

They watched the rest of the movie in complete silence.

Lisa's thoughts were racing a hundred miles an hour. She wanted to tell Eugene about her and Steve. She didn't know where to start. Her mind told her to tell him, but the words just wouldn't come out of her mouth. The movie ended and Eugene rewound the tape.

All the while, Lisa was just staring at him. Eugene caught her and said, "What is it, boo? You all staring at a nigga, you got something on your mind? Don't hold back. Speak your mind."

"Yeah, I do, but I don't know how to tell you."

"Tell me what?"

"If you let me, I might be able to tell you, but if I tell you, promise me that you won't get mad and you won't be mad at me."

"You got to tell me first, then I'll be able to tell you if I'm mad or not."

"Sorry, but you are going to have to promise me that you're not going to get mad or be mad at me before I tell you."

Eugene said, "Okay, fuck it, I'm not going to be mad at you, so you can go ahead and tell me. What is it?"

Lisa, feeling comfortable by now, opened up to Eugene. "Okay, but sit back down first." Eugene sat down next to Lisa, and she began spilling her guts. "Um, well it's like this, before we started dating or anything, I kind of was in a relationship with someone."

"So what? I'm not tripping that. I was in a relationship with Keyonna while we were dating. So what? You were in a relationship before we started dating."

"Baby, please, just hear me out because it is more to it than just that."

"Well okay, go ahead, Lisa, and tell me what's on your mind."

"Okay, like I said I was in a relationship with someone before we started dating and that someone was Steve."

"What?" Eugene sat straight up. "Steve who? Don't tell me…"

"Wait let me explain."

"Oh, hell no, I knew this was too good to be true. You're just like all the other bitches. How you gon' to try to play me like that?"

"Nigga, I'm trying to be honest with you."

"If you were being so honest, why didn't you tell me this shit before?

"Because I figured you would act the way that you are acting now."

"What the fuck you mean act the way I am acting now? You got me fucked up. Man, fuck this shit! I'm up out of here. You got motherfucking issues."

Lisa grabbed Eugene by his arm, pleading, "No, please don't leave. Don't leave me, baby. Please stay."

Eugene's facial expression said it all without him speaking, and then he said, "Get the fuck away from me before you make me do something to your dumb ass." Eugene walked out the door. As Eugene walked up the street to get to his house, he realized he left his back pack with his gun in it at Lisa's house, but his pride was too much in the way so he didn't want to go back to Lisa's house. He was thinking, *Damn, she used to fuck with that bitch-ass fool Steve. I can't believe it.* Eugene was so engaged in his thoughts that he didn't notice the car that circled around the block.

Steve, waiting his opportunity to catch Lil' Loc alone, he said, "Yeah, that's him, now we're going to see how hard this fool is now. Drive around the corner and come back around. We are going to serve this fool."

Steve's homies remarked, "Yeah, we are going to serve this fool."

Eugene was about a block away from Lisa's house when the car pulled up in front of him. Before Eugene could react, gunshots sailed at him. He tried to run, but he felt bullets hitting him. He didn't know where, but he was hit.

The car then screeched off. He felt a burning pain inside of him. He prayed that he would make it. Eugene crawled to someone's house and then he passed out. He didn't hear the commotion around him. Someone had already called the paramedics and the police was on the scene.

Around the corner…

Lisa heard the gunshots. First she didn't think nothing of it until she came out on her porch and saw a car speeding down the street. Immediately, she thought about Eugene. She ran up the street where there was a crowd of people gathered around with the paramedics and the police She tried to run under the yellow tape, but an officer stopped her.

She was crying and screaming, "What happened?"

Ms. Jackson, an elderly lady who used to watch Eugene and Lisa walking and holding hands, grabbed Lisa and told her that somebody had shot Eugene and that he was with the paramedics.

They were about to take Eugene to the hospital. They cut off his clothes and applied pressure to his wounds. They finally got the bleeding to slow down. Sirens were sounding as the paramedics were leaving the scene to rush Eugene to the hospital.

Ms. Jackson put her arms around Lisa and said, "Come on, Lisa, let me walk you home. That is just a damn shame what happened to that boy.

Lisa asked, "Who is going to tell his family what happened? They need to know where he is being taken."

Ms. Jackson replied, "I'm sure they will find out."

A squad car stopped in front of the Wilson's residence. Donte, James and Niesha are playing in the front. Whey the police officers got out of their car, Niesha ran in the house. "Ma, there's two police officers coming to the house!"

Mrs. Wilson jumped up and slipped into her robe. She headed for the front door. When she opened the door, she was faced by two officers.

Fear shot through her. She looked in the front year. All her kids were accounted for, except Eugene. A tight knot formed in her stomach.

"Oh my God," she whispered.

The officer said, "Hello Ma'am. I'm Officer Tucker and this is my partner Officer Jones, and we are from the 77th Homicide Division. May we come in?"

Mrs. Wilson was shaking like a leaf on a tree on a windy day. She stepped back and opened the door wider for them to enter. "Yes, come in. What is going on? I don't know why homicide would be visiting me."

Officer Tucker asked, "Ma'am, do you have a son by the name of Eugene John Gardner?"

"Yes, but what? Oh my Lord, please don't let it be, not Eugene."

"Ma'am, please calm down. For right now, everything is all right. Eugene was a victim of a drive-by shooting, which we believe to be gang-related. He's in the Emergency Trauma Center at Martin Luther King Jr. Hospital. They are working on him now. I just have a few questions that I would like to ask you. Do you know or have any idea if Eugene is affiliated with a gang?"

"Well no, Eugene is not in any gang. He knows I don't approve of that at all." Officer Tucker replied, "Well, Ma'am, I'm sorry for what has happened to your son and I hope he pulls through. Take care."

Both officers turned to leave. When they got into their squad car, Officer Jones said, "Why didn't you tell her that he is a gangbanger?"

"I couldn't tell her that. That would have really crushed her. You saw her. She has a lot to deal with."

"She is going to end up finding out anyway."

"You might be right, but not from me." Officer Tucker drove off.

Chapter X

~At The Hospital~

Eugene was in surgery from his gunshot wounds. Luckily for Eugene, the bullets penetrated through him. Dr. Hopkins went out to the lounge where Eugene's family was waiting to find out the details on his well-being.

Dr. Hopkins asked, "Who is here for Eugene Gardner?"

Mrs. Wilson shot up from her seat. "Yes."

The doctor hand motioned for her to remain seated. Everybody was there, all of Eugene's family, Lisa, Thea, Locsta, and many more. All was quiet as Dr. Hopkins spoke. "It seems that Eugene will make it. He is a very strong young man, not to mention blessed also because two of the gunshots he suffered were to the upper torso where he lost the most blood. It was hard to subdue those wounds and stop the bleeding. The rest of the gunshots were to his left leg and right shoulder blade. But like I said, he is a strong young man."

Mrs. Wilson asked, "When can we see him?"

Dr. Hopkins replied, "Well right now, he is resting from all the drugs we had to give him after the surgery, but you are welcome to go in and see him. Everyone else will have to wait until tomorrow."

Lisa spoke up, "What about me, doctor, can I see him please?"

"And who might you be, young lady?

"My name is Lisa, I'm his girl friend."

Dr. Hopkins told Lisa, "Since you are not immediate family, you will have to come back tomorrow. I'm sorry!"

"But, doctor…"

Mrs. Wilson said to Dr. Hopkins, "Please, let her come in with me to see him. I don't want to go in alone and what better person to come with me than Lisa?"

"Okay, this one time. The next time you will have to wait until visiting hours."

Lisa replied, "Thank you, doctor, and thank you Mrs. Wilson."

Some of the people waited and some left while Mrs. Wilson and Lisa went in to see Eugene. Mrs. Wilson and Lisa entered the room. Eugene was resting. Mrs. Wilson and Lisa pulled chairs close to the bed and they both sat and watched Eugene. After twenty minutes, Lisa stood up and walked over to the head of the bed. She stood over Eugene. Looking at all the monitors and tubes hooked up to him saddened her. She began to cry again.

She whispered in Eugene's ear. "Baby, I am so sorry. Please forgive me. I didn't mean for this to happen. Oh I am so sorry. Baby, I hope you hear me. I love you. You are going to be okay."

Mrs. Wilson just sat back and watched Lisa as she talked to Eugene. Mrs. Wilson finally got up and hugged Lisa and said, "Everything will be all right."

65

"No it won't. This is my entire fault."

"Girl, don't say that. This is not your fault. Those boys did this to my baby."

"No, you don't understand. I should have just told him and all of this probably would have never happened."

"Told him what? Girl what in God's name are you talking about?"

"Nothing, it's nothing."

Mrs. Wilson looked at Lisa in bewilderment and said, "Child, I think it's time that we leave. It's getting late and we got to get you home."

"But I want to stay with him."

"You can come back after school tomorrow. I'll come get you, if your mother says it's all right. But now, we have to go; besides he needs to rest and he'll be all right, okay honey?"

"Okay, but let me say bye to him first." Lisa leaned over and kissed Eugene and whispered in his ear, "Good night, Eugene. I love you."

Mrs. Wilson said her good-bye and they left.

When they returned to the lounge, they told everybody who stayed that Eugene was going to be okay.

For the first week Eugene was always resting. The second week he was awake and talking. One morning two detectives came to see Eugene to ask him some questions. Eugene was nervous because he didn't know what they wanted, but he remembered something his uncle had told him, which was to never talk to the police about anything, even if you get shot; you still play dumb.

The detectives walked in Eugene's room and sat down. He began his conversation with Eugene by saying, "I'm Detective Taylor and this is my partner Detective Williams, and we are from the 77th Homicide Investigation Unit. We would like to ask you some questions, okay?"

Eugene replied, "Okay"

"Are you Eugene John Gardner and were you born June 25th, 1983?"

Eugene replied, "Yes."

Detective continued, "This is just normal procedure, but I'm going to try to make this as simple as I can for you okay?"

"Okay," Eugene replied.

Detective Taylor asked, "Do you know the color of the car the shooters were driving?"

"No, I don't remember."

"Well, do you know or do you have any idea who did this to you?"

"No, I don't and what will make you think I do?"

Detective Williams, in an arrogant manner, said, "We think you are in a gang, and we know that this drive-by shooting is gang-related. We also know that they call you Lil' Loc on the streets, so stop wasting our time with your shenanigans."

Detective Taylor, trying to keep things calm, said, "Now calm down, Williams. See, Eugene, we are just trying to help you and we can only do that if you cooperate with us. So what is it going to be?"

Eugene began to open up to the detectives. "Well, I don't remember anything. All I know is that I am laying here in the hospital because someone or some of them shot me and y'all are making it sound like I did something wrong, when I didn't."

Detective Williams retorted, "Hold up here for a minute! I know a gangbanger when I see one, and who do you think you are getting smart with? All you little gang bangers are too big for your own britches and one day you will see it. I just hope that you are not in a box or in jail before you wake up and see that this is not the way. Take care of yourself, Eugene." Detectives Taylor and Williams walked out of Eugene's room.

In the car...

Detective Williams said, "It's a shame how these youngsters are today. These older Kats are leading them to destruction and they don't care. The youngsters think that it's cool when it isn't. Eugene seems like a good kid, but he is misguided and I just pray that he will wake up before it's too late."

Eugene continued to progress with his recovery and received lots of visitors. After six weeks, he was released from the hospital. Mrs. Wilson, Lisa and Donte picked him up from the hospital. As the nurse wheeled Eugene to the lounge to meet his family, she told him to try to stay out of the cold for at least another week or two. They reached the lounge where Eugene's family was waiting. Lisa ran and hugged him. Eugene hugged her back, but in his mind, he still couldn't get over what she had told him. But for now, he was going to play it cool. Mrs. Wilson walked to him and hugged him, but Eugene could see that she had this look in her eye. It was a look of disappointment. Donte and Eugene talked for a minute and then they all left the hospital. The doctor notified Mrs. Wilson that Eugene was to take his medication for pain twice a day for the next two weeks, and he was not to go outside in the cold for two weeks.

Chapter XI

~The Plot of Revenge~

*A*t *home…* Eugene, Donte and Lisa sat in the living room while Mrs. Wilson went downstairs to let Mr. Wilson know they were all back from the hospital. Mr. Wilson wanted to talk to Eugene about what happened and about what he was doing to himself and the people who cared about him. Mrs. Wilson came back upstairs and entered the living room.

"Your daddy wants to speak to you," she said to Eugene.

Donte and Lisa helped Eugene out of the wheel chair and helped walk him downstairs to Mr. Wilson's room. Mr. Wilson pointed towards the recliner chair and said, "Sit him right there in the recliner chair. Thank you both, y'all can go now."

Donte and Lisa went back upstairs.

"So, boy, how do you feel?"

"I feel all right. I get these pains, but other than that I'm all right."

"Well, the reason I want to speak to you is because I would like to know what's going on with you, son. How did you end up getting yourself shot up?"

"What do you mean by that?"

"What I mean is this, why would someone want to shoot you if you weren't involved in some type of nonsense that you are not supposed to be involved in? I know how it is for you kids today, especially you boys. Momma has been telling me about the incidents you have been involved in, you and your friends. Momma thinks it is another one of them phases that you are going through, but I know better and whether you admit it or not, I know and feel that you are in some type of gang or you are associated with people who are involved in a gang. Either way, it is both bad and you are headed down a dangerous road. And personally I am not going to have it and I don't want that nonsense around this family or me. Between you and Donte, y'all are something else and I refuse to let y'all worry Momma or me to our graves. I won't stand for it, Momma might, and you don't know how much you are hurting her. I'm not going for that either. So, either you get yourself right or you are going to have to go. I'm sorry, but I don't want no trouble brought to my house.

"We have these girls here and I don't won't any knuckleheaded hoodlum shooting my house up or the police kicking my door in on account of you or anyone else. I don't need that in my life. You understand me, boy?"

Eugene said in a whispered tone, "Yeah, I understand you. Is that it?"

"No. that's not all. I need to address one more thing; you got that girl Lisa all stressed out over you. I sure hope you don't get that girl into nothing. You don't know how you got her life in jeopardy, too. She could have been with you when the hoodlums shot you. Luckily she wasn't. Thank God for that. Boy, you better be careful."

Mr. Wilson yelled for Donte and Lisa to come help Eugene up and take him back upstairs. They took Eugene to his room, where he and Donte stayed so they could talk. Eugene told Lisa that he would talk to her later, so she left.

Donte asked, "What's cracking, lil' bro?

"Man, them fools tried to down me."

"I know, that shit was scary."

"I know. All I remember is these fools rolled up and started shooting. But the crazy thing is that I saw that same car earlier that day when me, Lisa and James were walking home from school."

"So are you saying that was the same car that shot you up?"

"Yeah. Man."

"Did you know who all was in the car?"

"No, but trip this, I was telling James that if that car come around again I was going to bust on them."

"So what does that have to do with anything?"

"If you hold on I'll tell you. Like I said, I told James that I was going to bust on the car if they came back around, but Lisa was like 'No baby, don't worry about them. Let's just hurry up and get to my house.' So that's what I did."

"Look, fool, that's still not saying anything"

"Okay, but trip this. When we got to her house, James kept walking, while me and Lisa inside her house. We kicked it and watched a movie. I felt her eyes on me when I got up from the couch to remove the tape. So I asked her was there something she wanted to get off her mind. For a minute she didn't know what to say. Then she asked me that if she told me would I promise that I won't get mad and that I wouldn't be mad at her."

"So what did you tell her?"

"At first I was like just tell me, then I'll let you know if I'm mad at you or not."

"But she wasn't going for that, right?"

"Right, so I promised her I wouldn't be mad at her. So she told me."

Donte, eager to get to the bottom of what happened, said, "She told you what, Eugene?"

"She basically told me that she used to fuck with that fool Steve."

"What? That nigga Steve from RBP?"

"Yeah that nigga."

Donte just shook his head in dismay. "Man, she was tripping. I know you flipped after that."

"Yeah I flipped so hard, I left my backpack with the strap in it at her house and that's when the fools rolled down on me."

"Hold up, man. You don't think that she had something to do with it do you?"

Eugene responded in a shameful manner. "Man, bro, I don't know, but I can say this much, if she didn't have anything to do with it, she sure knew that Steve was one of them dudes in the car."

"How do you know that?"

"You see, she knew I was going to dump those fools out. They probably would have come back around, so she saved him and didn't tell me shit."

"Okay, but what are you going to do?"

Eugene said in a pitiful voice, "Right now, I can't do anything but as soon as I get back on my feet, I'm going to get that fool Steve and then I'll deal with that bitch Lisa."

"You aren't going to do something to her, are you?"

"No, but I'm not going to fuck with her like that no more. As a matter of fact, we are over. She over here trying to make up because she fucked up, but it's too late for that. But first things first, and that's me getting better. I have to go to therapy and shit, but I guess it will help."

Eugene was getting healthier and was improving gradually. It took two weeks for him to get back to where he could walk on his own. It ended up taking Eugene a full month to completely recover.

Chapter XII

~Get Back~

Four months later…
Eugene went to school. As Mrs. Wilson dropped him off in front of the school, his homies were standing there. When they saw him get out of the car, they surrounded him, greeting him and telling him what's been going on since he had been in the hospital. Eugene already knew what had been going on because Donte already had put him up on the episodes that had been going on around the hood.

Devil Loc and Demon pulled Eugene to the side, so that they could holler at him away from everybody else.

Devil Loc asked, "What's up homie? You all right?"

"Yeah, I'm straight"

Demon chimed in. "Yeah, my nigga, we are here for you. We were at the hospital, too. You were out every time we came to see you."

"Those drugs they gave me had me fucked up."

Devil Loc said, "Yeah, we heard that bitch-ass fool Steve and his homies did that to you."

"Who told y'all that?"

Demon snapped back at Eugene. "Ah, man, don't trip. We got connections, and it was your brother. So are we going to ride on them niggas or what?"

"You know it."

Devil Loc put his two cents in. "I heard they been hanging tough since they shot you. We was going to go serve them fools, but Locsta, Spooks and Looney was like let's wait until you get out the hospital and back on your feet. Now that you're back, we can go lay those fools down. They were hanging on the Avenue at this fool name K-Bo's house. He just got out of Y.A. So they were kicking it with him."

Eugene said, "Is that right? Well look, after school, meet me at Wacky's house. I'm going to hit my brother on the hip and tell him to come, too. Until then, I'll holler at y'all."

Devil Loc asked, "Hey, my nigga, what's going on with you and Lisa?"

Eugene responded," Nothing, I'm cool on her right now. Why, what's happening?"

"Nothing, I was just asking that's all because y'all were hell of tight before you get shot up and now, y'all don't even talk to each other."

"It's nothing though."

"For sho', my nigga. I'll holler."

Demon spoke up. "Yeah, we'll holler. One love, my nigga."

At lunch…

Eugene and his homies were sitting at the tables when Thea approached and asked Eugene, "Can I speak with you?"

"Okay, what's cracking with you, Thea?"

"I'm doing all right, but what's going on with you and my girl? You got her bugging. She told me that she told you about her and Steve."

"Yeah, is that right? Well I guess you know that she was fucking with him before me."

Thea said remorsefully, "Yeah, but it wasn't my place to tell you anything. Plus she was going to tell you anyway."

"Yeah almost one year later."

"I guess she felt it would take that long."

Eugene retorted, "That's bullshit and you know it."

"Look y'all should just talk, because you got my girl all fucked up in the head. You know how she feels about you, so stop acting like that."

"Acting like what? Just tell her I don't want to talk right now. I got too much on my mind."

"Yeah, whatever, nigga."

"Okay, I see how you feel."

"You damn right. You want to play games and shit, you should be grateful that she told you because she didn't have to. And if you're blaming her for you getting shot up, you need to stop because you know that nigga was going to try to get you anyway."

"Yeah, you're right, but still I don't feel like talking so I'll holler at Lisa when the time is right."

Eugene went back to the table with his homies. As Thea was leaving, Keyonna walked up to the table to say hi to Eugene. Thea never looked back to see Keyonna at the table talking to Eugene. When Thea reached Lisa and their friends, Tiffany walked up all excited.

Tiffany asked, "Girl do you see that?"

Thea responded, "See what?"

Tiffany said, "Is that Keyonna over there talking to Lisa's man?"

Lisa then looked over and saw Keyonna smiling and laughing.

Thea said, "Oh hell no, we going to fuck that bitch up. She knows that y'all are still together."

Lisa started to cry as she walked off. Thea chased her down. "It's going to be okay. That nigga ain't nothing to trip off of."

Lisa asked, "Why is he doing me like this? All I did was try to be honest with him. He got me twisted. Fuck this shit."

Back at the table...

Eugene and Keyonna were just chopping it up having a friendly conversation when Lisa, Thea and their friends started walking towards the table. Eugene was so much engaged in a conversation with Keyonna that he didn't notice them until they were right there.

Lisa asked, "Eugene it's like that? You just going to talk to this bitch in my face?"

Keyonna said, "Bitch! Who are you calling a bitch, Lisa?"

"You, bitch." Then Lisa walked over to Keyonna and slapped her. The two of them start to fight. Thea tried to jump in but Demon grabbed her while Eugene broke up the fight. They fought for a while, but once they started pulling each other's hair, Eugene decided to break up the fight. Both Lisa and Keyonna were breathing hard. Eugene asked Keyonna if she was all right. She replied yeah, and left. Eugene held Lisa and then he walked her to another table far away from everyone else.

Eugene asked," Girl what's wrong with you?"

Lisa snapped, "Nigga, what's wrong with you? Are you trying to get back with that bitch? I know she still likes you."

Eugene responded, "You're tripping. You need to stop listening to your friends because I know one of them bitches told you some bullshit. Keyonna is just my friend. Just because she is my ex-girlfriend don't mean we can't speak to each other.

So before you start jumping to conclusions, find out the facts."

"Well how was I to know? Lisa asked. "You haven't spoken to me since you been home from the hospital."

Eugene said, "It's been a lot of stuff on my mind and I have to take care of things."

"But, baby, you can at least talk to me. Baby, is it over between us? If so I don't want it to be."

Eugene paused and then said, "I don't know."

Lisa said to Eugene in an apologetic way, "Baby, I need you. I'm sorry for not telling you about Steve and me." Lisa started to cry. She said, "I promise I will never hold anything back from you again. I love you and I want to be with you and you only."

Eugene said, "All right, we'll see what's cracking. But for now, what made you get off on Keyonna like that?"

"I was stating my prize and I had to show her who was you number one girl."

Eugene smiled and said, "That's right, boo. I have to watch you. You pack a mean little punch."

Lisa smiled, and said, "Yeah, you better watch out because next time it might be you that I get off on."

Eugene laughed hard and said, "Is that right? I know you're talking about something else, because you know you can't whoop me." The bell sounded and they walked off to their next class.

Throughout the rest of the day, Eugene had thoughts of how he was going to lay that fool Steve down. That was his main concern—Steve, his target. Eugene was so far involved in his thoughts that he didn't hear the bell sound for school to end.

Locsta, Demon, Devil Loc, Spooks, Looney, Scrappy, Puppet, Post, Wacky and Lil' Wacky were waiting on him when he exited the school. Lisa ran to catch him. When she did, she found him with his homies.

Lisa said to Eugene, "Baby, hold on a minute."

Eugene responded. "What's cracking, boo? I'm about to go to the home's house. I holler at you later, all right?"

"Okay, but as soon as you get home call me."

"All right." He gives Lisa a kiss and leaves with his homies.

At Wacky's house…

As soon as they entered Wacky's house, Eugene picked up the phone to page his brother so he could come to Wacky's house, too.

Wacky said, "So what's cracking Lil' Loc?"

"You know me, my nigga, ready to take care of business as usual."

Locsta replied, "Yeah, that's why a nigga wanted to wait for you because I know that you would want to be a part of this."

Lil' Loc responded in an exciting manner, "And you know it!"

The phone rang. Wacky answered the phone, and it's Donte. Wacky handed the phone to Eugene.

Eugene answered the phone. "Yeah, what's cracking, bro?"

Donte said, "I'm on my way right now. I'll be there in about three minutes."

"All right, nigga, we'll be here. One!"

Donte repeated, "Yeah, one!"

Eugene went back into the living room with the rest of his homies. Eugene said, "Yeah, that was bro."

Locsta asked, "What homie talking about?"

"He's on his way. He should be here in a minute."

As they all waited for Donte, they started to hear loud music being played. The music was coming from a car outside.

Locsta said, "Man, who is that beating like that?"

Eugene said, "I don't know, but whoever it is, it is knocking. Matter of fact, let's go see."

They all walked outside to see who was the person banging the loud music. The car pulled up to Wacky's house and stopped. Then Donte got out the car.

Eugene said, "Damn, nigga, where did you get this motherfucker from?"

"I bought this from Dogg."

Locsta chimed in. "You bought the beat from Dogg, too."

"No, I got my shit hooked up at Auto Sounds. Anyway, what's the business?"

Wacky said, "Let's go back inside so we can holler. As a matter of fact, y'all meet me in the garage."

"All right, let's move," Eugene said.

They all walked to the garage so they could fill Donte in on the business.

Locsta said, "Peep game, my nigga, it's like this. We know where this fool, Steve live, and who he be fucking with."

Donte said, "Yeah, for sho'. That's the business, so when are we going to do the due?"

"We are going to do it tonight, bro," Eugene said with much eagerness. "This fool Steve was acting like it's all good when it ain't. He is going to pay with his life tonight."

Devil Loc chimed in. "Yeah, that's right, my nigga. Fuck him and his homies. All those bitch-ass niggas and bitches are going to die tonight."

Eugene stood up waving his hand and said, "Hey, calm down my nigga."

Locsta went on to say, "Anyway, like I was saying, we know where this nigga be hanging out at. He is at the Soda Pop a lot, like every Friday he is there and he is going to be there tonight. It starts at 7:00 pm and ends at 1:00 am in the morning. But Steve and his homies leave at 11:30. They do that all the time. After they leave the Soda Pop they go straight to his house with some bitches. He don't even be paying attention."

Wacky said, "Yeah, he don't bother to check if somebody is following him or not. He feels hell of comfortable, so much that he is slipping. We followed him one night, just to test it out and neither him nor his boys knew we were on they bitch asses."

Locsta said, "That's the business, so until then, we just going to kick it. Wait till it is time to handle the business."

Devil Loc, all ready for the shit to go down, said while laughing, "Well, Lil' Loc, my nigga, fire that blunt up, homie."

Lil' Loc sparked the blunt and said, "Here, my nigga. He passes the blunt to Devil Loc, and said, "We got about two hours before the Soda Pop starts."

Lil' Loc decided to call Lisa and see what she was up to. Lil' Loc went inside the house to use the phone. He dialed Lisa, and she picked up on the first ring.

"Hello."

"What's up, boo? What are you doing?"

"I'm chilling, just getting ready."

"What are you getting ready for? Are you going out?"

"Yeah, me and Thea and some of the girls were thinking about going out."

"That's cool. Where y'all planning on going?"

"We were thinking about going to the Soda Pop."

In Lil' Loc's mind, he was thinking, *Damn*. He said, "Is that right! Why there?"

"We haven't been there in a minute, so we wanted to go see what's cracking. If you don't want me to go then I'll holler at the girls and we'll go somewhere else."

"No, do your thing. Go have some fun. I want you to enjoy yourself."

"Okay, and what about you? What are you going to do to night?"

Lil' Loc thought to himself, *You don't want to know this truth.* "Shit, I'm just going to kick back and fuck with my brother and the homies."

"That's cool. Why don't y'all just come to the Soda Pop?"

"Oh, No! We cool. A nigga really ain't trying to go out tonight."

"You know it won't be the same without you there."

"Yeah, I know, but maybe next time. I was calling to see what's happening with you. Now that I know, I'm going to holler back."

"Okay. I love you, baby."

"I love you, too, boo."

Lil' Loc went back to the garage with his homies. Lil' Loc said to his homies, "Check game, my niggas. Lisa and her girls are going to be at the Soda Pop tonight."

Locsta shouted, "What? Did you tell her not to go?"

"No, for what? We are going to get this nigga Steve. I don't want her to get all suspicious and shit."

Wacky questioned, "But what if that nigga Steve see her in the motherfucker?"

Lil' Loc retorted, "So what?"

"Look, man, I'm just saying, if he see her, in which I'm pretty sure he will, he's going to automatically think that you're there."

"Hold up," said Locsta. "This might work to our benefit."

Wacky replied, "Fool, what are you talking about?"

"If he thinks that Lil' Loc is there then he might turn around and leave."

Wacky said, "The nigga might stay, too. You know how he be feeling himself."

Locsta said, "Yeah, that's just a gamble we're going to have to take."

Lil' Loc replied, "It really don't matter to me, I'm ready to dump this bitch-ass nigga out in broad daylight."

7:35 p.m.

The Soda Pop is cracking and the line is long. Lisa, Thea and their friends are waiting to get in, and they are looking good, especially Lisa. She is super fly, wearing a black and red DKNY dress with the jacket, purse and boots to match. Thea is dressed identical to Lisa, but in a blue and white DKNY dress, white jacket, purse and boots. All the Kats are staring at them and whispering. As they get to the door, they pay the fee and enter, but not before getting a compliment from the bouncer. They thanked him, smiled and go inside.

When they got to the dance floor, on their way to the table, the DJ was playing that "Freak Ho's" by Luke.

About 8:45 pm, Steve and his clique pulled up to the Soda Pop. They parked and got out, making their way to the club.

Steve said. "It's going down tonight."

K-Bo responded, "Yeah, my nigga. It's packed. Let's hurry up and get up in there." They paid and entered the club.

As Steve and his homies entered the club, it's barely enough room for people to move around. Steve said, "Damn, homie, it's tight up in here."

K-Bo responded, "Yeah, I know. It's barely room to move, but it's cracking."

Steve said, "You said that right!"

They continued to squeeze their way through when they came across three fine females. Steve, K-Bo and Sleep decided to approach the females and ask them to dance. The females accepted their proposal and danced with them. They all danced together for three songs straight before they decided to take a break. They went to the bar and everyone ordered a bottle of water. Twenty minutes later, Steve, K-Bo and Sleep decided it was time to get back to the party.

Across the dance floor...

"Say man, is that Steve and his homies?"

2nd party said, "Yeah that's them bitch-ass fools."

1st party said, "Oh yeah, it's on tonight."

Unknown to Steve and his homies, they had other niggas out for him because they were moving into their territory. The other guys were from G.M. and they were not feeling Steve.

12:37 am…

It's getting close to closing and there were a lot of people at the exit trying to leave and beat the rush. Lisa, Thea and their friends were also trying to exit early. As the exiting started to flow, people were leaving out. Lisa and her friends finally made it outside, and they bumped into Steve and his homies.

Steve said, "Damn, watch where you're going, bitch!"

Lisa looked at him with disgust and said, "Fuck you, nigga"

Steve laughed and said, "You already did that."

"Oh I can't stand you!"

Steve smiled. And as they were walking away he turned around and said, "So, how is Lil' Loc? I haven't heard anything on him yet." Steve and his homies continued to their cars. As they reached the cars and got in, there's a commotion in front of the club. The two guys from G.M. are arguing with these girls that got them blocked in front of the exit.

Around the way…

Locsta called out, "Okay Lil' Loc, y'all ready?"

"Yeah, they just came out," Lil' Loc said. "Let's do this."

Lil' Loc, Locsta, Demon, Devil Loc, Puppet, Scrappy and Donte got out of the two vans and walked around to where Steve and his homies were. Wacky and Post were the drivers, so they stayed behind with the vans running. Steve and his homies were three cars deep. Steve, K-Bo, Sleep and Throw-Down were in Steve's car.

Lil' Loc made the first move and then everyone else followed. Lil' Loc leveled the 9mm on Steve and pulled the trigger. Gunshots rang out all guns. Lil' Loc and his homies made it back to Wacky's house where they changed clothes. Then they got rid of the guns, dumped the vans and everyone departed. The whole area at the club was taped off. There were no survivors of the three cars. The next day, it was front-page news: 12 DEAD AT A TEENAGE NIGHTCLUB. NO SUSPECTS HAVE BEEN ARRESTED AND SO FAR THERE WERE NO WITNESSES.

Chapter XIII

~Summer~

It's been about eight or nine months since the Soda Pop Night Club incident, and people have been carrying on with their lives as normal. No one is certain about what took place on that night at the club where twelve people lost their lives. Rumors circulated about what happened; some think it could have been some members from G.M. because they overheard someone talking about serving Steve and his homies a few weeks before the incident occurred, which was cool with them because they went about their everyday lives like nothing ever happened.

It was about to be summer break from school and everyone was so excited, especially Lil' Loc. This was the summer where he really got to get his clown and ball on. His Uncle Will was going to help him put his car together. Lil' Loc had bought an '83 Monte Carlo from his lick money. Every day he and his uncle would go to get the necessary parts that he needed to put his car together. Instead of buying a car that was already hooked up, Lil' Loc wanted to put a car together himself, with the help of his uncle. This took place in the month of June and Lil' Loc wanted everything to be completed by the beginning of July. He wanted to be able to drive the car for the rest of the summer. His uncle assured him that they would be finished by then. When school was out, Lil' Loc and his uncle worked on the car every day. Eugene and his uncle were coming along fine with putting the car together. Eugene spent the majority of his afternoons and nights at his uncle's house working on his car.

One week later...

Finally, school was out so that gave Eugene more time to work with his uncle on the car. At the rate they were going, they would be finished before Eugene's birthday, which was June 28. The body of the car was finally completed. They started working on the engine of the car. Eugene wanted a fast car, so his uncle was making sure he got just that. He was going to have the engine so souped up that no other Monte Carlo could match it. After about a month and a half of working on the car, it was finally completed. The engine was hot, and the beat was knocking. All Eugene had to do was get the car painted and put on the rims.

He took the car to Jay's Paint Shop to get the wet candy color paint on the car. Eugene wanted a color that would stand out, so he got candy green apple paint. He thought that would look banging with the twenty-inch rims. This all took place two days before his seventeenth birthday. You know Eugene couldn't wait to show his new car off two days later on his birthday. It was Eugene's birthday and he had been amped up all day. His family and friends were giving him a party at the Hilton Hotel. They had rented out the ballroom, which could hold up to two hundred people, with a private DJ and catering service. Eugene felt his party was going to be off the hook.

While everyone was preparing for the party, and helping out with the set-up, Eugene, Uncle Will and Donte went to the paint shop so Eugene could pick up his car. Jack, one of the guys who painted the car, led Eugene to his car. When Eugene laid eyes on his car, he thought, *Damn, my shit is tight!* All excited, he opened the door and sat in the driver's seat. He clutched the wood grain steering wheel. Eugene then asked if he could start the car inside the shop. Jack said yeah. Eugene started the car and popped in one of his CDs, and it was sounding hell of good.

Donte and his uncle walked in and said, "Damn, you are in the game."

Eugene was ready to go, so he paid Jack for the paint job and they left.

Donte was riding with Eugene, while his uncle followed behind them. Eugene was speeding up Western Avenue with his car shining and the gold rims blinging. Uncle Will signaled for Eugene to slow down and pull over, so Eugene did just that.

Eugene asked, "What's up unc?"

"Eugene, you have got to slow down. I know you're excited and all, but I know you aren't trying to get your car impounded and you just got it."

"Yeah, you're right. I'll slow down Uncle Will. Matter of fact, let's get off this busy street and get to the house, so we can get ready."

"Okay. You follow me now."

"Okay, unc." Eugene followed his uncle to the house.

At Uncle Will's house...

Eugene and Uncle Will parked their cars. Eugene parked in front of the house, while Uncle Will parked in the driveway. As they walked to the house, Uncle Will's kids ran outside to greet him. He hugged and kissed them. The kids then ran over to Eugene and Donte and hugged them. They also said happy birthday to Eugene. They wanted to see Eugene's new car. He showed them the car and they liked it. They went into the house to get ready for Eugene's birthday party. Eugene wanted to drive his new car to his party, but his uncle l was against it, so Eugene rode with Uncle Will in his truck. Uncle Will had a Navigator on twenty-two-inch rims, and it was tight. At last they were ready to go. After all, the party couldn't start without the guest of honor...Eugene!

At Eugene's Birthday Party...

Everyone was prepared and in position at the party. As soon as Eugene and his family walked through the ballroom doors, everyone screamed, "H A P P Y   B I R T H D A Y!!!" The music started playing, signifying that the party had officially started. After several of Eugene's homies gave their greetings, Lisa approached Eugene and grabbed his hand to lead him to the dance floor. Eugene and Lisa turned the party out. They danced all night. Everybody surrounded them and was cheering them on. When the tempo slowed down, all couples were on the dance floor. Lisa said, "Baby, I can stay in your arms forever."

Eugene said, "Me too, boo."

"I love you, baby."

"I love you, too, boo. You know you're my number one, right?"

"Yeah, I know, baby. I got something to tell you."

"Okay, spit it out."

"Well, I'm pregnant."

"Is that right? Damn!"

Lisa was stunned at his response. All she could say to him was, "What?"

Eugene sensed in her voice that she was feeling disappointed by his reaction. He said to her, "Baby it's just that it's been a hell of a year. That's probably why I was feeling ill about a week ago. You're pregnant? How far along are you?"

"I'm three weeks."

"I'm going to be a daddy, damn!"

"So you're all right with it?

"Yeah. What, you don't want to have the baby?"

"You know I do. It's just that I didn't know how you would have felt about it."

"Well, now you know." The two of them kissed. "Do you want to let everyone know now?"

"I don't know. It's up to you. Whatever you want to do is fine with me."

So Eugene walked over to the DJ booth and told the DJ to kill the music. The DJ killed the music and Eugene walked over to the front of the stage on the dance floor. He signaled for Lisa to come up front with him. Now everybody was looking around, wondering what was going on. Eugene called to have everyone's attention. Eugene announced to the crowd, "If I may have your attention for a minute, I would like to make a toast. Drink, please!" Eugene was given two champagne glasses. "Okay, does everyone have a glass? Well first of all, Mom, Uncle Will, Donte, sis and my niggas, step up, please. Thank you. Y'all have always been here for me, even when I was down and when I was up and I love y'all for that. Today is a special day for me, not only is it my birthday, but I also found out that Lisa is pregnant…" he paused, as Mrs. Wilson passes out. He looked over to make sure she was being tended to before continuing. "…and I will be a daddy soon. So I toast to the future." Everyone toasted to Lisa's and Eugene's news.

Mrs. Wilson came to and sipped on some water. She told Eugene and Lisa to come near her. Mrs. Wilson said, "Boy and girl, y'all know that y'all are making a big step when it comes to you and that baby you are carrying."

Lisa replied, "Well Mrs. Wilson, the doctor said that I might be carrying twins."

"Twins? Oh lord! Well if this is something that y'all sure y'all want to do, then I support y'all one hundred percent. Girl, what your momma say about this?"

"She's disappointed, but she is okay with it. She's against abortions."

Mrs. Wilson said, "Well y'all have a long future ahead of y'all, but until then, I suggest you two celebrate this night fully.

Once that kid or kids get here, y'all hands are going to be full, so enjoy. I'm going home. This night was just too much for me."

Eugene and Lisa hugged and kissed. Mrs. Wilson then said good night. Then they went to sit down at the table. Several people came over and congratulated them. The night ended with a bang for Eugene.

Chapter XIV

~Lisa~

The next day...
The day consisted of Eugene taking Lisa to her doctor's appointment. He also took her shopping to make sure she had the right foods and the proper nutrition for her and the baby or babies. This went on for two months before Lisa found out that she was indeed carrying twins. Lisa's mother, Mrs. Wilson and some friends started early planning a baby shower that was going to be at Lisa's house. Lisa and Eugene went to the doctor so Lisa could get an ultrasound to find out if she was having boys or girls or both. The ultrasound read it was two boys.

They were having two boys. Eugene could barely conceal his excitement. He got on his cell phone and called everyone to let them know that they were having twin boys. Lisa's mother and Mrs. Wilson got the news and they were waiting for them to get back. Everyone was waiting for Eugene and Lisa at Lisa's house to get back from the doctor's office. They both were excited about the fact that they were going to have twin boys.

As they pulled into the driveway of Lisa's house, Eugene asked Lisa, "What's up with all them out there?"

"I didn't know."

Eugene let it go and the two of them got out the car and headed into the house. As Lisa put the key in the door, turned the knob and opened the door, everyone screamed, "CONGRATULATIONS on the twin boys!!!" They all hugged Eugene and Lisa.

The days went by smoothly with Eugene and Lisa spending more time together and taking care of business with the doctor's appointments. By them being potential parents and being teen parents, they enrolled in parenting classes. Actually, Lisa insisted on it.

It was 7:50 a.m., and Lisa woke up to the smell of bacon and sausage. She was surely hungry. Ever since she became pregnant, she was eating a lot, especially since she was having twins. As she rose, she looked over at Eugene to see that he was still sound asleep. They had made passionate love the night before, which consisted of a lot of foreplay and oh what a night! Lisa just stared at Eugene for a while and she knew then she was madly in love with him. She leaned over and kissed him lightly on the forehead. She got out of bed to go see what her mother was cooking in the kitchen.

Thirty minutes later…

Lisa walked into the kitchen and saw her mother scrambling eggs. She saw sausage in a pan on the table and she grabbed one. Lisa said, "Good morning," between bites.

Lisa's mom responded, "Good morning, sweetheart. I see you're up early."

"Well, I have to get the day started."

Lisa's mom was laughing as she commented, "After all that noise y'all was making last night, I thought your day was going to start a little late. But you know you got that young blood in you."

"What's that suppose to mean, Mom?"

Lisa's mother chuckled and said, "I'm saying that we know how to put it on him."

Lisa laughed. "Mom, you are crazy."

"So where is Eugene? He's still sleeping, I suppose."

"Yes. That's the way I left him." They both laughed.

Lisa and her mother sat down to eat. After eating, Lisa fixed a healthy plate and took it to her room for Eugene. When Lisa entered the room with the plate of food, she found that Eugene was up. She gave him his plate so he could eat.

"Aren't you going to eat, too?" Eugene asked.

"I have already had breakfast, so I am going to help Mom out with the dishes."

"Okay."

But before Lisa left, she took a piece of bacon off Eugene's plate and walked out the bedroom. But not before she heard Eugene calling her greedy. Breakfast was good. They had scrambled eggs with ham and cheese, bacon, sausage links, buttermilk biscuits smothered potatoes, and a big glass of ice-cold Tropicana orange juice. After breakfast, they all cleaned up. Eugene and Lisa bathed and got ready to go to the mall to do some shopping and catch a movie. The movie was starting at 1:35 pm. Eugene and Lisa enjoyed their movie and did some shopping.

The End of Summer

Summer was coming to an end and school would be starting back in September. Eugene and Lisa were prepared to go back to school. Lisa was going to be taking home study in November, since she would be almost six months in her pregnancy. September came and Eugene and Lisa went back to school. School was starting to get real boring for Eugene, plus he was missing the block. It had been a while since he had been on the block with his homies. Eugene decided to leave school early and hit the block. He would come back and pick up Lisa when school was out.

On the block…

Eugene bent the corner to the block and saw his homies chilling. He pulled up and stopped the car and got out. Everyone was saying, "What's up?"

Eugene exchanged greetings with his homies. "What's up with my homies?" Eugene walked to Wacky's front yard.

Devil Loc approached Eugene and said, "Lil' Loc, what's up with you, homie? You haven't been in the hood in a minute. Shit been happening and you been M-I-A."

Lil' Loc took off on Devil Loc and they started fighting. They fight for about two minutes before Locsta and Spooks break up the fight. Lil' Loc said to Devil Loc, "Nigga, I don't owe you or nobody any explanations."

Devil Loc repositioned himself and in a calm tone, he replied, "My nigga, shit just haven't been the same without you here. I know you are about to be a daddy and all, but, my nigga, the hood needs you." Lil' Loc's homies all nodded their heads in agreement with Devil Loc.

"Nigga, I'm going to always represent. Love and ride for the hood, y'all know that. Shit is just happening too fast, but anyway I'm here, my niggas. What's cracking?"

Lil' Loc and his homies chilled until it was time for him to pick up Lisa from school. That's how Eugene spent his days, hanging on the block and picking Lisa up from school. Eventually Eugene dropped out of school and spent his time on the block hustling, banging and doing a lot of other things. He was caught up in that life again. Lisa didn't say anything about it, but she noticed the change in Eugene just as well as others did.

November 22nd, three days before Thanksgiving Day...

Eugene and Lisa caught a plane to Denver to spend Thanksgiving with her family and do a little sightseeing. Eugene and Lisa hadn't really been talking as often as they used to. Lisa thought Eugene was distracting himself from everybody. She had been hearing about some of the things he was doing in the hood. The plane arrived in Denver after about four hours.

Chapter XV

~The Trip to Denver~

Eugene and Lisa were excited that the plane had landed. They walked inside the airport to meet Lisa's cousins who were picking them up from the airport. As they walked through the airport, Lisa spotted her cousins Tammy and Monica. She motioned to Eugene, and he followed Lisa to meet her cousins. Lisa hugged her cousins and made small talk with them. When her cousins saw Eugene, they said hello. They picked up Eugene and Lisa's luggage and walked outside where a Ford Expedition was waiting for them. The drive from the airport to Lisa's cousin's house was long, but it was a nice ride. Tammy and Monica lived in a middle-class neighborhood with both of their parents. Tammy and Monica are sisters with two younger brothers. Tammy was eighteen and Monica was seventeen, the same age as Lisa. They all were pretty close, especially Lisa and Monica.

They arrived at the house an hour and fifteen minutes later. Eugene took the luggage out of the truck and followed the girls inside the house. The boys, Marcus and Robert, were playing with their PlayStation, while Lisa's aunt was preparing dinner. They said hi to Eugene and Lisa. Tammy told Lisa and Eugene to follow her so she could show them to their room. The house was pretty big. It had six bedrooms and three bathrooms. They had a huge den and a patio in the backyard. They had it going on, not to mention how exquisite the kitchen looked.

Lisa's aunt (who everyone called Aunt Rose, because she seemed to make life blossom) told Lisa and Eugene to freshen up for dinner after they finished unpacking. Lisa and Eugene unpacked their clothes and went to freshen up. By the time Lisa and Eugene finished, Aunt Rose's husband was home from work. Everyone was ready for dinner. It was tradition for Lisa's family to sit down at the table together and have dinner. At the dinner table, they all bowed their heads in prayer, while Lisa's uncle blessed the food. Then they began to eat.

As they were eating and passing food around, there was casual talk going on. Talk about Lisa getting bigger and showing more; talk about the Thanksgiving feast that would be at Aunt Rose's house and more family and friends will be coming for the Thanksgiving feast. After dinner they had dessert. The girls cleared the table and did the dishes, while Lisa's Uncle Tim and Eugene sat in the den and talked until it was time for bed.

When Eugene entered the bedroom to prepare for bed, Lisa was just putting her nightgown on. Eugene took his shorts off and Lisa got a glimpse of something that looked like a tattoo on Eugene's stomach.

Lisa said, "Baby what's that?"

"What's what?"

"What's on your stomach? Is that a tattoo?"

"Yeah."

"Let me see it"

When Lisa saw what it said, she was astounded. Eugene had a tattoo of his neighborhood in large block letters on his stomach. Lisa asked Eugene, "Why did you do that?"

"Because I wanted to, so stop tripping and let it go. If it makes you feel better I have your name tattooed across my chest, right on my heart. So you know you have my heart and you will always have it. I hold you dear, right here." He pointed at his heart, where Lisa's name is tattooed. Lisa then hugged Eugene and apologized to him and said she loved him, and they both went to bed.

The next day, November 23rd...

Everyone woke up to the sound of Anita Baker playing on the stereo and to Aunt Rose singing, and of course the aroma of food cooking. Aunt Rose then announced that everyone needed to get up, wash up and come to the kitchen for breakfast. After everyone dragged themselves out of bed to wash up, they headed to the kitchen for breakfast. Aunt Rose continued to sing to Anita Baker as she set the table.

Everyone finally got themselves together and went to the table for breakfast. Uncle Tim did a morning prayer and everyone started to eat. Before anyone left the table, Aunt Rose informed everyone that they all were going to see Big Momma, Lisa's grandmother, later that evening at the nursing home. She also said that Big Momma would be spending the day and night, so she could be at home for Thanksgiving Day. Aunt Rose told Lisa that Big Momma really wanted to see her and meet Eugene. They all got dressed and went to see Big Momma at the nursing home. They had about a thirty-minute drive to the nursing home.

At the nursing home…

They arrived at the nursing home and everyone got out of the truck to go inside to see Big Momma. They waited while Aunt Rose signed them in, then they were escorted to Big Momma's living quarters. Big Momma was sitting by the window in her wheelchair. They all went to hug her and say hello. Big Momma was smiling and very happy to see her family.

Aunt Rose was closest to Big Momma, so she said, "Look, look Momma, look who we brought."

When Big Momma saw Lisa, she lit up like Christmas lights. Big Momma said, "Come here, sweetie, oh look at you…you looking all pretty. What you got cooking in the oven, girl? You sure are looking big."

Aunt Rose said, "Yeah, Momma, Lisa is having twin boys."

Big Momma said, "Oh girl, the Lord has surely blessed you. These are my great grandbabies in there."

Lisa smiled and said, "Yes Ma'am."

Big Momma asked, "Now where's that boyfriend of yours that helped you get this way?"

Lisa pointed and said, "He's right here."

Big Momma looked at Eugene and said, "Boy, come here so I can get a good look at you."

Eugene walked up in front of Big Momma. She smiled and said, "Well now, you are a handsome fella." Everyone chuckled. "You sure do know how to pick' em, Lisa, don't you? You have a name?"

"Yes, it's Eugene, Ma'am."

Big Momma laughed as she uttered out, "Well I be damn, you got manners."

"Yes, he does, Big Momma," Lisa said.

"Look at you, girl, standing up for your boyfriend. I like that. Now, as I was saying, Eugene, well that's a strong name. I remember I had a boyfriend named Eugene in my day. He sure was a nice and decent fella, too." Big Momma then told Eugene to lean forward. When Eugene leaned forward, Big Momma whispered something in his ear. When she finished, Eugene stood up. He smiled at Big Momma and nodded his head and said, "Yes, I will."

Big Momma told Eugene to take care of Lisa and those babies. They all had a good time spending time with Big Momma. Before they left, Aunt Rose told Big Momma that she would be back tomorrow morning to pick her up. Big Momma told her to make certain that she brought Lisa and Eugene with her.

Everyone was up early and at work getting the house prepared for Big Momma and Thanksgiving. While they did that, Aunt Rose, Lisa and Eugene were on their way to pick up Big Momma from the nursing home. They arrived at the nursing home twenty-five minutes later. Aunt Rose signed Big Momma out, while Lisa pushed Big Momma in her wheel chair and Eugene carried her bags. They helped Big Momma into the truck, in which she wanted to sit in the back with Eugene, so Lisa rode in the front passenger seat. They made small talk all the way to the house. There were going to be a lot of guests, family and friends coming in later that night and everyone were going to stay at Aunt Rose's house. They got to the house and Eugene helped Big Momma into her wheelchair, then Lisa wheeled Big Momma up the ramp and into the house. Eugene grabbed Big Momma's bags to bring in. When Aunt Rose entered the house, Tammy told her that Uncle James called to let them know that they were at the airport. Aunt Rose and Tammy went to pick them up from the airport. The rest of the family and friends would arrive later. They were driving from Nevada.

Everyone finally arrived and they were all together. There were a total of twenty-one people in a six-bedroom house. It was going to be a tight fit. Big Momma slept in the room with Marcus, everybody else slept wherever they could find a spot.

Thanksgiving Day...

People woke up having to step over each other and some even got stepped on. Eventually, everyone was waking up trying to get in and out of the bathroom, which was like rush hour on the freeway. Somehow they all managed to wash up. The three bathrooms came in handy. The women and young women helped everybody with breakfast by giving everyone cereal, so they could start preparing the real feast for the day. Eugene and Big Momma talked some more. He also met all of Lisa's other family members and close friends of the family.

Eugene decided to call his family and friends to say Happy Thanksgiving. He called Mrs. Wilson first to say Happy Thanksgiving to her. When he finished talking to Mrs. Wilson, he talked to his brother, Donte.

Donte said. "What's up, lil' bro?"

"Just chilling. Happy Thanksgiving."

"Yeah, you, too. When are you coming back?"

"I'll be back soon. Why? What's happening?"

"I'll holler at you when you get back home. Enjoy yourself.

"Okay."

Eugene then called Uncle Will who answered on the first ring. "Hello."

"Unc, what's up? Happy Thanksgiving."

"Same to you, nephew. How are things going out there for you in Denver?"

"It's going cool, but I miss y'all. How are the kids?"

"They are good, running wild like usual. They miss you, we all do. Look, nephew, when you get back slow down for me."

"Why you say that?

"Well, I guess you didn't hear."

"Hear what?"

"Lil' Post and Lil' Puppet got killed two days ago."

Eugene went silent for a moment. He could not believe that he had heard correctly. Then he said, "Unc, what?"

"Yeah, nephew, it's been going down out here on these streets.

"Damn, Unc, when are they going to have the funerals?"

"I heard it was going to be on the 30th for Lil' Post and on the 1st for Lil' Puppet." "I'll be there. "

"When are you coming back?"

"Our tickets are for the 29th"

"Well okay, I'll see you then. Tell Lisa I said hello."

"Okay. Tell the wifey and the kids I said I love them and Happy Thanksgiving."

"Nephew, keep your head up. I love you."

"I love you, too, Unc."

Eugene came out the room trying not to look distraught, but Lisa spotted him and saw that something was wrong. "Baby, are you okay?"

"I'm all right."

Lisa caught him by his arm and said, "Let's go in the room." She pulled him into the room and locked the door. Lisa knew that something was very wrong and she wanted to get to the bottom of what was bothering Eugene. "Now baby, tell me what's wrong and don't say nothing."

"They killed the homies."

"What homies? What are you talking about?"

Eugene said, with much sadness, "I'm talking about Lil' Post and Lil' Puppet."

"Oh my God, damn, baby, I'm sorry."

"Well, no need to trip about it now. I just have to wait to get back to Los Angeles, so let's have a nice Thanksgiving."

The evening came and went. Everyone got full and laughed and had a good time. Eugene tried his best to enjoy the evening, but what was on his mind was the loss of two of his homies and those who did it, would surely pay.

For the rest of the time spent in Denver, Eugene was just focusing on revenge and getting back, so he couldn't wait to get back home. Everyone said their good-byes and Aunt Rose, Tammy and Monica drove Lisa and Eugene to the airport. They arrived at the airport an hour before their flight, so Aunt Rose, Tammy and Monica waited with them. They made small talk, which made the time go by, until it was time for them to board their plane. Eugene and Lisa's flight number was called. They all said their good-byes again and departed.

Eugene and Lisa boarded their plane to Los Angeles, California. Eugene's mind was wondering like he was in a trance. The flight to LAX was going to take about three and a half hours.

Chapter XVI

~Casualty~

Eugene and Lisa arrived at Lax after a long and exhausting flight. Lisa's mother was there to pick them up. Eugene and Lisa got their luggage and walked out of the airport to meet Lisa's mother who was waiting out front. Eugene put their luggage in the trunk of the car and got in the back seat. Lisa's mom asked how their trip was and how was their Thanksgiving. Lisa told her it was excellent. Lisa and her mother made small talk about the trip while Eugene was lost in his own thoughts. It didn't take long for Eugene to doze off and take a nap. Before he knew it, Lisa was waking him up telling him that they were home, at his house. He got his bags and hugged and kissed Lisa and her mom and told Lisa to call him when she got home. He walked inside the house as they drove off.

Inside the house, everyone was running around Eugene, yelling that he was home. Mrs. Wilson called for him. She was in the kitchen, so he went into the kitchen.

Eugene said, "Hi, Ma."

"Hey baby. How was your trip?"

"It was okay. I had a wonderful time. I met a lot of Lisa's family."

"Yeah, how is Lisa doing? Is she handling the pregnancy well?"

"Yeah. Sometimes she is uptight, but overall she's handling it pretty well."

After Eugene helped Mrs. Wilson with the dishes, she asked him if he was going to the funeral tomorrow for Keith? (Lil' Post). He said yes. Mrs. Wilson also knew about the funeral services planned for Larry (Lil' Puppet) as well. After talking and helping Mrs. Wilson in the kitchen, Eugene went to his room.

Donte came in about ten minutes later. "Man, what's up, my nigga?"

"Shit, not too much. I am just trying to get my thoughts together."

"I feel you! But let me fill you in on what happened with the homies."

Eugene was very anxious to hear what the real deal was. "Okay."

"What happened was…that night y'all left to go to Denver, the homies and me went to the 7 to 7 (7:00 pm to 7:00 am) at the skating ring. While we were doing our thing, that fool Squeak and Lil' Scrooge and a few of their homies and some bitches came in."

"I know Squeak, that nigga is from G.M."

"Yeah, bro. Okay so Squeak and his homies are in. Me, Lil' Post and Lil' Puppet were chilling in the center circle, and them bitches came up and grabbed Lil' Puppet by the hand and ask him to dance. My nigga, the bitches were bold! So she and Lil' Puppet dance for like three songs, then she whispered in the homie's ear. Next thing I know they were leaving the circle."

Eugene could hardly wait to hear the whole story, he asked, "So what happened?"

"Well, the homie was gone for about fifteen minutes and when he came back he was sweating and wiping his face. We asked him what happened and he told Lil' Post and me that he and baby girl went to the bathroom and he hit. So we were chilling when all of a sudden those fools, Squeak, Lil' Scrooge and their homies come through the circle and they push up on us. Squeak, Lil' Scrooge and the bitch that the homie hit approaches Lil' Puppet and Squeak and asked Lil' Scrooge is that him? Lil' Scrooge replied yes. Lil' Scrooge saw Lil' Puppet and the bitch go into the bathroom and the bitch was Squeak's girl."

Eugene clenched his fist and with a deep frown said, "What?"

"Yeah, the homie hit Squeak's bitch."

Eugene wanted every detail. "What happened after that?"

"After Squeak, Lil' Scrooge and his bitch approach the homie and Lil' Scrooge told Squeak that Puppet is the one who fucked Teresa, in which she denied, that fool Squeak slapped the bitch. Then he tried to bang on the homie, in which Lil' Puppet wasn't going for that. Lil' Puppet told Squeak that 'This is 2DC and fuck you.' Lil' Puppet got off on Squeak and when that happened, Lil' Post and I jumped in and somebody yelled to his homie that we were fighting, and they jumped in, too. We smashed Squeak and his homies.

"The security kicked us all out and called the police. So we all got in our cars and left. We went to the hood and posted."

Eugene asked, "So where do Squeak play a part in the homie getting killed?"

"Let me get to that and you will see. The next day, while we were on the block, Lil' Puppet and Lil' Post went to the burger stand and you know how they like to walk through the alley...I guess they saw them walking through the alley and knew they were going to go back that way so they waited. When the homies went back that way them niggas killed the homies." Donte started to cry. Even Eugene started to get teary-eyed.

Eugene remarked, "So you are saying that Squeak and Lil' Scrooge killed the homies?"

"I'm not saying it. I know they did it because it couldn't have been anybody else. Plus since we took out them RBP niggas, them G.M. fools been trying to cross their boundaries. So I know they did it. We haven't got them yet, but we did down five of their homies so far. It's war!"

Eugene replied, "You damn right! I got them fools Squeak and Lil' Scrooge. You ready for the funeral tomorrow?"

"Yeah. The homies missed you and is going to be happy to see you, even at a time like this."

Eugene said, "Well for sho'. You know what you wearing tomorrow?"

"Yeah. We are all wearing shirts with Lil' Post's picture on it. It's hooked up. I got you one and I got you one for the homie Puppet's funeral, too."

"All right, let's get some sleep. We have a big day ahead of us."

"All right in the morning."

The day of Lil' Post's funeral...

Eugene and Donte woke up at 7:15 am. They got their clothes together for the funeral, which were black khakis to go with the black t-shirts and black Chuck Taylor All Stars with the fat laces. They were going to be dressed alike accept Donte, he was going to be wearing blue Chuck Taylor All Starts with the fat laces. They ate first then showered and got dressed. They were going to take Eugene's car. Eugene had to pick up Lisa, so she could go, too. Eugene drove to Lisa's house to pick her up. She was waiting on him as he pulled into the driveway. Donte got out and got in the backseat, so Lisa could ride in the front seat with Eugene. The funeral was going to start at 9:30 am, and they had about twenty-five minutes to get there. Lil' Post's momma wanted the funeral at Saint Baptist Church and the burial will be at Inglewood Cemetery.

They arrived at Saint Baptist Church to find that everyone was there already and parking was limited. They parked and walked to the church. There was a long line of people waiting to get in the church. Eugene spotted some of the homies in the front of the line. He yelled to them and they told him to come up there with them. When they got up front they greeted one another and entered the church. Before sitting down, they signed the book for Lil' Post and got an obituary. As they were looking for seats, Lil' Post's mother saw Eugene. He walked over and gave her a hug and told her that he was sorry. She started to cry. She then asked Eugene to sit in the front with her, so he did. Everyone was coming to pay their respect to Lil' Post's mother as they viewed Lil' Post. The funeral service started and it was a good service. Lil' Post was laid to rest right.

After the funeral service and the burial, everyone went to Lil' Post's mother's house where people ate, sat around and talked about Lil' Post. They all tried to remember the good times with him. For Eugene and his homies they knew that they had to go through this again tomorrow. Eugene and his homies said their good-byes to Lil' Post's mother. But before going home they went to meet at Shorty Loc's house to discuss business. Before going to Shorty Loc's house, Eugene dropped Lisa off at home.

Chapter XVII

~ Pay Back & Arrests~

At Shorty Loc's house…

Eugene arrived at Shorty Loc's house to find all of his homies gathered up. When he parked his car and got out, two of the homies started fighting. Eugene walked up to them and pushed one of them back. Eugene asked, "What the fuck is wrong with y'all?"

One of the homies (Taz) who was fighting said, "Man, Lil' Loc, fuck that fool. He don't be putting in any work and that fool don't be in the hood anyway."

Eugene said, "So what Taz? Kick back. This is the night of the homies' funeral. If anything, we should be squaring up to go serve them G.M. niggas."

Locsta stepped in and said, "Yeah you're right, homie. Niggas is just emotional and shit. We had Lil' Post's funeral today and tomorrow we are having Lil' Puppet's funeral. We just fucked up."

Eugene said, "Well, we are going to get nothing out of whooping on each other. So since niggas are on one. Let's go serve them G.M. niggas." Taz and TC, who both recently got put on, were about to go on their first mission. "Taz, Shorty Loc and TC come with me."

Locsta said, "Donte, Devil Loc and Demon, we're riding out. Wacky, Post, Puppet and Scrappy, we're together."

So with that said and done, they all went three car-loads full to go serve them G.M. niggas. As they all went around the corner to one of the houses that the G.M.s were hanging at, they heard loud music being played. They all stopped and Lil' Loc signaled to Locsta to come here. When Locsta approach Lil' Loc, Lil' Loc told Locsta that they (GM's) were having a house party, and that they were going to park and walk up to the house as if they were going to the party. Locsta said, "Okay." He went to let Wacky and the rest of the homies know the new plan. They all got out of their cars and walked the short distance to the house where the party was taking place. As they all got in front of the house, they all pulled their guns out and started shooting.

They all ran back to their cars and left. The next day in the newspaper, it mentioned the incident of the shooting: THREE WERE DEAD, SEVERAL WERE WOUNDED AND THERE WERE NO SUSPECTS IN CUSTODY OR ANY WITNESSES THAT WERE WILLING TO COME FORWARD. Lil' Loc showed Locsta and Donte the newspaper. They all tripped off it for a minute and laughed. Lil' Loc said, "Damn, my niggas, we stay making the newspaper."

Funeral Number Two

They all got ready for Lil' Puppet's funeral, which pretty much went the same as Lil' Post's funeral service. The only difference was that at Lil' Puppet's mother's house, his mother was really tripping. She was talking to Lil' Loc because she knew him better than she knew any of the other homies. Lil' Puppet's mother, between tears, she said, "Eugene, why my baby? Oh my baby is gone. I don't know what I'm going to do. They killed my baby."

Eugene hugged her and said, "I'm sorry! It's going to be all right."

Lil' Puppet's mother asked, "How? How is it going to be all right? My baby is gone."

Eugene told her, "I can't bring Larry back, but I can promise you that I will get them fools who did this."

Lil' Puppet's mother started screaming and shaking like a leaf on tree. She said, "No, No, just leave it alone. I have had enough. My baby is gone due to that and no matter what, it just isn't right. Y'all can't continue to go on like this. The Lord don't approve of it. But why did He take my baby?"

Eugene said, "Calm down, Ms. T."

Lil' Puppet's mother remarked, "I can't, oh Eugene promise me you will not try to revenge my son's death."

"I can't do that, Ms. T."

Lil' Puppet's mother shouted loudly, "Leave, just leave. I want you out of my house. It's your fault anyway. It's all you no-good gangbangers' fault that my baby is in the ground, so all y'all leave! Get out!"

Eugene told the homies, "Come on y'all. Ms. T. is really tripping, let's bounce. All the 2DC's leave."

Eugene and his homies go to Wacky's house where they start drinking and smoking marijuana, just chilling. Out the clear blue sky Demon goes on one. Demon yelled out, "Fuck this shit, homie. I am about to go lay some of them G.M. fools down."

Devil Loc jumped in. "Yeah, me too!"

Lil' Loc told them to chill.

Demon said, "Chill for what? I'm tired of chilling. I'm ready to lay somebody down."

Lil' Loc replied, "Hold up, fool, we just laid some of them fools last night, so kick back. I'm pretty sure they know it was us or think it was."

Demon retorted, "So what? Them fools aren't just going to get away with what they did."

Lil' Loc was getting pissed; he snapped back, "They ain't got away with shit!"

Demon shouted, "I'm on one, who's with me?"

Lil' Loc said, "Nigga, we all with you. I'm just saying hold down."

"Fuck that. I'm supposed to ride when you are ready to ride, hell no!"

Lil' Loc said, "Look, fool, you're tripping and you bugging out, so you know what? I don't expect you or nobody else to jump when I say jump, but I'm just trying to get you to be smart for a second, but go ahead and do your thing."

"I'm going to," Demon responded.

Devil Loc spoke up, "I'm going with you."

"Me too," Demon and Devil Loc said.

Scrappy chimed in "Yeah, I'm in, too."

Demon asked, "The rest of y'all straight?" Everyone else remained silent. Demon said, "All right then, let's move."

As Demon, Devil Loc, and Scrappy pulled off to go serve the G.M. Kats, they didn't know that the G.M. Kats were expecting and waiting for some of the 2DC's to come through. When they went through G.M. territory, they ended up having a shootout with each other and they had a high-speed chase with the police. They ended up crashing into a corner store, so they bolted out the car and ran. They were all caught and booked on attempted murder charges.

News about the arrest and what happened to Demon, Devil Loc, and Scrappy got back to the hood that night while everyone was still at Wacky's house. It was a large scene in the G.M. hood. The police and ambulances were everywhere. Police officers were asking people all types of questions, but no one was talking. Demon, Devil Loc, and Scrappy were booked and sent to juvenile hall on attempted murder charges. Things around the hood were quiet for about three weeks.

Three weeks later...

Locsta and Lil' Loc were riding around in Locsta's car listening to the sounds when they stopped at a red light. Lil' Loc looked to his right and noticed a familiar car sitting in the drive thru of a fast food restaurant. He tapped Locsta and told him to look at the car. The car was a Brougham Cadillac.

Lil' Loc said, "That look like Squeak's car."

"Yeah it sure does. Let's turn around so we can get a closer look."

Locsta turned around when the light changed. As they got closer, they realized that it was Squeak and Lil' Scrooge and two females in the car.

Lil' Loc said, "Yeah, that's them and they are slipping."

"Yeah, we got them. Let's pull around in the alley. They parked in the alley and got out of the car. They had the upper hand because Squeak's car was blocked. There was a car in front of him and one behind him in the drive thru. Lil' Loc and Locsta put a black rag over their nose and mouth to cover most of their faces and they put a beanie on and pulled it down low. Now they were ready. They walked towards their car.

Once they reached Squeak's car, Lil' Loc said, "What's up now?" But before Squeak or Lil' Scrooge could react their bodies were riddled with bullets.

Squeak fell on the steering wheel sounding the horn. The two females started screaming. The murder of Squeak and Lil' Scrooge made headlines in the newspapers, saying that they were murdered in cold blood in front of their girlfriends in broad daylight. The article further read if anyone had information on the whereabouts of the two cold-blooded killers to contact police at once. It was also the talk throughout many neighborhoods, because Squeak and Lil' Scrooge were well-respected with reputations. Lil' Loc and Locsta were laying low for a while.

About four months after the death of Squeak and Lil' Scrooge, two members from G.M. and Teresa (Squeak's girlfriend and baby momma) walked into the police station. They were escorted to Detective Taylor's desk. Detective Taylor gestured for them to sit down.

Detective Taylor asked, "So how can I help you all today?"

G.M. member 1 said, "Well first off we are only here because we would like for justice to be served."

Detective Taylor asked, "How can I help you so we can make sure that justice will be served?"

G.M. member 1 replied, "Also, we want to make sure that after we tell you this, we will be okay."

Detective Taylor remarked, "I can assure that you will be okay. We have one of the best witness protection programs."

G.M. member 1 said, "Well tell him what you told us."

Teresa began by saying, "Well, um, the day that my boyfriend got killed."

Detective Taylor interrupted her, "Hold up. Wait, wait a minute, let me get my pad and pen. Now, who is your boyfriend?"

Teresa replied, "My boyfriend was Clarence Tony aka Squeak."

Detective Taylor said, "Oh okay. I'm sorry about what happened, but continue."

Teresa continued talking. "I was with him and Lil' Scrooge and my friend. She doesn't want to come forward. Anyway the two guys who shot and killed them, well one of them yelled 'What's up now?' before he shot his gun."

Detective Taylor looked a little confused. "Okay, so what does that have to do with anything? Can you identify the shooter?"

Teresa answered, "No, but I did recall hearing that voice before and it sounded like Lil' Loc."

"Lil' Loc, I know him. I dealt with him before. Oh yes, he was a victim of a drive-by shooting a year or two ago. Are you sure about the voice being the voice of this Lil' Loc?"

"Yes, and also someone got a license plate number and gave it to me."

Detective Taylor was getting more interested now. "You have a license plate number and you've been holding on to it? Why didn't you come forward before now?"

G.M. member 2 spoke up. "She was afraid. Plus we told her not to say anything it's the code of the streets. But now, we are just fed up and we want something done. So that's why we are here. So are you going to help up or what?"

Detective Taylor nodded his head and said, "Yeah, leave me all your information, and whatever else you all have and I will get on this right away."

They left all the necessary information and Teresa gave him the paper with the license plate number on it. Detective Taylor told them that he would contact them and that they will be called upon in the future.

Detective Taylor went to his partner and they went up to the captain's office. On the way to the captain's office, Detective

Taylor told his partner that he got a lead in the Tony/Smith case with some new developments. They entered the captain's office and Detective Taylor explained the situation and the new developments to the captain. When the captain learned about the new developments, he congratulated the two detectives and told them to get right on it and "Let's bring the perps in." They went to do what they were ordered to do and by the end of that day, they had enough evidence that they could obtain a warrant for the arrest of Eugene Gardner aka Lil' Loc and Donald Brown aka Locsta.

At Locsta house…
Locsta was in bed sleeping when he heard a hard knock at the door. Then they heard a voice. "Open up, this is the police!"

Locsta's mom opened the door and the police charged in telling everyone to get down. The officer asked, "Ma'am, where is Donald?"

Locsta's mom asked, "Why y'all want him? What did he do?"

Officer replied, "He's running."

Locsta had jumped out of the window, but it was no use because his house was surrounded. Locsta was caught and was arrested. The detective explained to Locsta's mother that he was a murder suspect and that his car was spotted during the time a murder was committed.

At Lil' Loc's house…
There was a hard knock at the door. Mrs. Wilson went to see who was at the door. She opened the door and it was the police.

She started to panic as she asked, "What is going on?" The officer didn't pay her any mind. They were barging in rooms and making everyone get out. They put Donte down and cuffed him. Mrs. Wilson was asking them, what do you have him for?" When Detective Williams saw him he told the officers that Donte wasn't him, so they un-cuffed him.

Detective Williams asked, "Where is your son Eugene?"

Mrs. Wilson responded, "I don't know. Why? What's going on?"

Detective Williams said, "If you know the whereabouts of Eugene, it's important that you contact my partner or me immediately."

Mrs. Wilson asked again, "What are you looking for Eugene for?"

"He is a suspect in a double murder case."

The detective and officers left mad and disappointed. Mrs. Wilson was in shock and she didn't know how to take what she had just heard. "Eugene a murder suspect? Oh my God, No! After all that has happened it can't be true."

Donte called Lisa's house and asked to speak to Eugene. Eugene came to the phone and said, "Hello."

Donte said, "Check this out, bro; the police just hit the house looking for you."

"What? For what?"

"They said you are a murder suspect!"

Eugene said with much surprise, "Damn!"

"You better lay low. Ma is over here messed up."

Eugene, trembling in his voice, said, "Did anybody say where I am?"

"Hell no! You know we would never do that. Kick back and stay low. One!"

"Yeah one!"

Eugene remained on the run for about three weeks. He was driving one day with Taz, Shorty Loc and Tails in the car. When they approached a red light and stopped. A police car pulled up on the side of them and started to stare at them. Lil' Loc tried to remain calm, but he was nervous. Instead of waiting for the light to change to green he tried to run by speeding off.

They were blindsided by a bus and the car spent into a light pole. It was a big accident. The police witnessed the entire incident and radioed it in. The only survivor from the accident was Lil' Loc, but he sustained injuries that were life threatening. He was hauled from the totaled car and rushed to the hospital where the doctors began immediate surgery on Eugene. He suffered from a severe head injury, broken leg and arm and three fractured ribs. After surgery, Eugene was placed in ICU. The doctors didn't know if Eugene was going to make it or not. However, Eugene did survive. The doctors said it would take Eugene a few months to recover but he'd be all right.

The detectives wanted to arrest Eugene, but the doctor told them that they would have to wait. An officer was placed outside of Eugene's door at all times and he wasn't allowed any visitors. A few weeks later, Eugene woke up to find two detectives sitting at his bedside.

Detective Taylor said, "Well look who is awake. It's good to see that you are awake so we can get on with it. First I'd like to have the honor of reading you your rights. You have the right to remain silent. Anything you say can and will be used against you in a court of law. You have the right to an attorney. If you cannot afford an attorney, one will be appointed to you. Do you understand these rights?" Eugene didn't say anything. Detective Taylor continued. "Well, I take that you do. What about your partner? Doesn't he know his rights?"

Detective Williams said, "Yes. I take it he does."

Detective Taylor spoke up. "Well, you fucked up Lil' Loc. We got you, and let me tell you something you will go down for this. I'll be back in about a week or two to take you to the station and book you. We can't start without you. We've got your buddy."

Two weeks later the doctor released Eugene and the detectives were there to pick him up. They handcuffed him to the arm of his wheel chair and wheeled him to the car. Eugene left the hospital with his arm and left leg in a cast.

Detective Taylor placed a phone call to the Wilson's residence. Mrs. Wilson answered the phone.

"Hello."

Detective Taylor said, "Yes, is Mrs. Wilson in?"

"This is Mrs. Wilson Speaking. My I ask who's calling?"

"This is Detective Taylor from the homicide division."

"Oh, how may I help you?"

"I know you are aware of your son's accident."

"Yes I am."

"Well I just wanted to notify you that he is okay and that we have arrested him and he is being charged for murder."

Mrs. Wilson was speechless for a moment then she said, "Oh my God, What?"

"Eugene is being booked right now in Los Padrinos Juvenile Hall for murder. Sorry to bring you such bad news, Mrs. Wilson."

Mrs. Wilson was so shaken up from the news she'd just heard that she started having hard time breathing. Mr. Wilson tried to help her regain her composure. He called for Niesha to come downstairs. Niesha ran downstairs to see what was going on.

"Get Momma some water. She's upset about something," Mr. Wilson said.

"Okay." She went to the kitchen and poured Mrs. Wilson some water and took it to her. Mrs. Wilson drank the water and started to feel a little better. Niesha asked, "What's wrong, Momma?"

Mrs. Wilson spoke in between sips of water and her sobbing. "They got Eugene locked up on murder charges."

Mr. Wilson and Niesha asked at the same time, "On what charges?"

"Murder charges! That detective man, Mr. Taylor, just called and told me."

Niesha inquired, "How did that happen when Eugene was in the hospital?"

Mrs. Wilson said, "I don't know how or when, but that's what that detective man said. We just have to find out what's going on."

Mrs. Wilson asked Niesha to call Lisa and tell her to come over to the house. Niesha got the phone and dialed Lisa's number.

"Hello."

"Lisa, this is Niesha."

Lisa cheerfully said, "Oh hey, girl. What's going on?"

"Well, Ma, wanted you to come over to the house right now!"

Lisa asked, "Is she okay? What's going on?"

"Just come to the house, please!"

Lisa, feeling quite nervous, did not want to ask any more questions, so she said, "Okay I'm on my way."

Niesha said, "Lisa is on her way, Mom."

Mrs. Wilson said, "Okay. Thank you, sweetie."

Back at Lisa's house…

Lisa called her mother and asked her to take her to Mrs. Wilson's house. Lisa's mother said, "Yes sweetie I will happy to do that for you." She sensed that something was wrong but she did not ask Lisa any questions. Lisa and her mother got in the car and headed to Mrs. Wilson's house. At eight months pregnant, Lisa was moving slowly. Lisa and her mother arrived at Mrs. Wilson house ten minutes later.

Donte answered the door bell. "Who is it?"

"It's me, Lisa"

Donte responded, "Oh okay."

Donte opened the door for Lisa. She entered the house and asked where Mrs. Wilson was.

"She's downstairs," Donte told Lisa.

Lisa slowly walked down the stairs to Mrs. Wilson's room to find Mrs. Wilson, Mr. Wilson and Niesha all sitting close together. Lisa said, "Hi, Ma."

"Hi, baby. Come here, we need to talk."

Lisa sat down next to Mrs. Wilson. Mrs. Wilson trying to remain calm, said, "Lisa, I want you to prepare yourself for what I am about to tell you."

Lisa, feeling nervous, asked, "Ma, what's going on? Is something wrong?"

Mrs. Wilson replied, "Yes it is. Do you remember that detective man, Taylor?"

"Yes."

"Well he called me today and he told me that they have arrested Eugene for murder."

Lisa screamed. "Oh my God, no!" Lisa started to cry uncontrollably and got very emotional. Mrs. Wilson held her and told Lisa to try to keep it together. All types of things was racing through Lisa's mind, so she didn't hear Mrs. Wilson talking to her.

Mrs. Wilson shook Lisa and asked, "Lisa, girl, do you hear me?"

Lisa, holding on to Mrs. Wilson, said, "Oh excuse me, Ma. What did you say?"

"I said that Eugene was arrested on murder charges!"

"I heard you, Ma. I just can't believe that this is happening."

"Neither can I, but we have to be strong through this, especially you for the sake of those babies."

"You're right, Ma, it's just that everything seemed to turn around drastically."

"I agree, but now we got to figure out what's going on with Eugene and how we can help him out of this situation. Eugene should be calling soon. I know that he's allowed a phone call." Just as Mrs. Wilson said that, the phone rings. Mrs. Wilson answered the phone, "Hello."

The operator spoke. "You have a collect call from Eugene. If you wish to accept this call please press 5 now." Mrs. Wilson pressed the number 5 on the phone. "Your call is being accepted."

Eugene said, "Hello"

Mrs. Wilson responded, "Hi, baby."

Eugene spoke very softly. "Ma I don't know what's going on, but they came and got me from the hospital telling me they got me on murder charges, when I haven't done anything."

Mrs. Wilson, trying to act calm, said, "I know, baby. That detective man, Mr. Taylor, called and told me that you were arrested on murder charges."

"Yeah, what else did he say?"

"That was all he said."

"Okay. Well I go to court in three days at the Compton Court for arraignment."

Mrs. Wilson, sobbing, but trying to keep Eugene from knowing, said, "We will be there."

"Okay. Does Lisa know?"

"Yes, she is right here now. Hold on I'm going to give her the phone"

Lisa says, "Hey, baby!"

"Hey, boo. They got me in here on some bullshit. How are you holding up?"

Lisa said, "I'm a little better now that I'm talking to you. Baby, I don't know what I would do if I lose you." Lisa started to cry.

Eugene, holding back a tear himself, said, "Baby, calm down. It's going to be all right because this is some bullshit. They don't have anything on me, plus they got Locsta, too. He's in the county jail."

"Damn, baby, they are trying to say you killed some people."

"I know, baby, but they are on some bullshit. I didn't kill anybody."

"I believe you, boo. When do you go to court?"

"I go to court in three days. I have to get off the phone. I love you. Tell ma, Mr. Wilson, Niesha and Donte I love them, too."

"Okay. I love you, too.

Chapter XVIII

~Trial & Victory~

Three days later...

Mrs. Wilson, Lisa and the rest of Eugene's family were in the Compton Court to hear what the judge was going to say about the charges against Eugene. Eugene walked into the courtroom and sat behind the table with his public defender.

As the judge walked into the courtroom, the bailiff said, "All rise!" Once the judge is on the bench, the bailiff said, "Please be seated." He then announced, "Honorable Judge Weatherbe, presiding."

Judge Weatherbe said, "Hello counselors," speaking to the District Attorney and to Eugene's Public Defender. Judge Weatherbe continued, "Today is just a day where the defendant, Eugene John Gardner, is being arraigned on two counts of murder and two counts of gang enhancement. The preliminary hearing is set for thirty calendar days from today, which would be December 12." The bailiff called the next case.

Lisa was hysterical. Mrs. Wilson did her best to calm her down. She told Lisa that she was going to get Eugene a lawyer because she was not going to let her baby get stuck in jail for life. Eugene was in a world of trouble and Mrs. Wilson wanted to make sure that he had a fair chance. For about a week she searched for a good criminal lawyer. She spoke to several attorneys regarding Eugene's case. Finally she came across a lawyer that caught her interest, an attorney by the name of Sam Zokeski of Zokeski and Lander Law Firm. Mrs. Wilson was in the law office with Mr. Zokeski discussing Eugene's situation.

Mrs. Wilson asked, "How are you, Mr. Zokeski?"

"I'm doing fairly well, just another busy day. How may I assist you?

"Well, my son has been charged with murder."

"Murder?"

"Yes. He is a juvenile, but I'm pretty sure they are going to try him as an adult.

"I will have to find out what's going on with him. When is his next court date?"

"It's December 12."

"Okay, well my fee to represent Eugene will be $5,000.00. You will need to make a deposit of $2,500.00. After the court date, when I find out what's going on, like as far as the evidence they have against him and I have a chance to read his file, I will let you know the additional charges. Meaning, if this case goes to trial or not."

"Okay, will you take a check?"

"Yes. You can make the check payable to me."

Mrs. Wilson wrote the check in the amount of $2,500.00 made payable to Mr. Zokeski, and handed him the check.

"Thank you, Mrs. Wilson, and I will see you in court on the 12th of December. Oh, and it might be better if Eugene got tried as an adult. Do you know if he has a co-defendant?"

"What's a co-defendant?"

"A co-defendant is a crime partner or someone who has committed a crime with Eugene."

"Oh yes. Eugene does have a co-defendant."

"Okay, is he a juvenile or an adult?"

"I think he is an adult, because I didn't see him with Eugene in court."

"Well I will know more on the 12th."

"Thank you, Mr. Zokeski, and it's an honor to have you on my son's case."

Mrs. Wilson left the attorney's office smiling and feeling a lot better after she talked with Mr. Zokeski. As she arrived home, everyone was outside waiting on her to get back.

Donte spoke first. "Hey, Ma, how did it go?"

"It went very well. I like this lawyer. I have a good feeling about him."

"Yes, that's what's up because my bro don't need to be in there."

"I know baby. Where is Lisa?"

"She's lying down. She has been very tired and you know she's about ready to bust."

"Yes she is. Okay, I'm going in the house to check on her."
Mrs. Wilson entered the house and went to the bedroom where
Lisa was lying down. Mrs. Wilson said to Lisa, "Baby, get up."

"Huh?"

"Lisa, how are you?"

"I'm find, Ma."

"How's my grandbabies?"

"They are fine, just been kicking me all day."

"They have? Well they are ready to get out of there."

"Yes they are."

"Anyway, I went to speak to an attorney by the name of Sam
Zokeski and he seems to be very good."

"That's good, Ma," said Lisa. "Does he cost a lot?"

"Yes, but he's well worth it. Did Eugene call?"

"Yes and we talked for a while today. I miss him so much.
Every time I think about him I just want to cry. I don't know what
I would do if I lost him." Lisa started to sob.

"Now gain your composure, girl. Eugene needs you to be
strong for him and the twins."

"Your right, Ma, but it just hurts to not be able to see him."

"I know, sweetie, but that's what we are here for to support
each other and help each other get through this. That's what family
is all about."

"Thank you, Ma, for all the support," Lisa said.

Mrs. Wilson hugged Lisa. "Girl, you are family and like I said
that's what families do."

Mrs. Wilson and Lisa continued to talk for a while then Mrs. Wilson got up and told Lisa that she's going to cook and check on Mr. Wilson. They hugged and Mrs. Wilson left the room to go do her motherly and wifely duties.

Mrs. Wilson cooked and cleaned the house. She made sure everyone was fed and taken care of before she decided to eat and retire to her room to rest because today was a long and exhausting day for her. The next day and days to follow consisted of everyone busying themselves and being very supportive of Lisa.

Eugene was a mess. He was stressing hard while being locked up. He was fighting almost every day. He was housed in a H.R.O. unit, which was a high-risk offenders unit. The unit was E-F; the staff that ran the unit was pretty cool. They didn't bother you unless you were a total jerk who just acted out all the time. One day, while sitting in the dayroom eating chow, Eugene was at the end of the table when an inmate asked him where was he from? The inmate asked, "Hey, what's up? Where are you from?"

Eugene responded, "What Loc, this is Westside 2DC."

Inmate said, "Oh, I know who you are. You are Lil' Loc."

"I don't know you. Where are you from?" Eugene asked.

"I'm from G.M."

Eugene then yelled disrespectful things to the inmate from G.M. as he jumped out his seat and rushed the inmate from G.M. who was his rival. They fight for about a minute before the staff rushed in the dayroom with pepper spray drawn and ordered Eugene and the inmate to stop fighting. Once the staff got the situation under control, they locked down the remaining inmates.

Eugene and the inmate he was fighting went to the box. The box is a room with no bed, just a mattress on the floor and you are in complete isolation. When you have a fight you go to the box for seventy-two hours, but for Eugene it would be longer because this wasn't his first time going to the box and Eugene was considered a fuck up.

A fuck up is an inmate who fails to obey the rules of the institution or detention center. Everything Eugene was doing while incarcerated was being documented and reported to the court. That's how it was for Eugene during lock up. He was fighting because he refused to be labeled as a buster, so he made sure people knew that he was a rider and that he was going to represent his neighborhood to the fullest.

Two days before court, Lisa woke up from hard kicks from the twins. She tried to get up, but the pains were overwhelming. Lisa yelled for Mrs. Wilson. As soon as Mrs. Wilson reached the room, Lisa's water broke. She was going into labor.

Mrs. Wilson said, "Breathe Lisa!"

Mrs. Wilson told Niesha to go start the van because Lisa was going into labor and they had to rush her to the hospital. Mrs. Wilson helped Lisa up and called for Donte to help her get Lisa into the van. They drove to Abel Freeman Hospital, where Lisa gave birth to healthy boys, who weighed in at six pounds, five ounces and nineteen inches. Yes, Lisa was truly excited. She named the boys James and John Eugene Gardner. Lisa was so exhausted after giving birth to the twins that she passed out. The nurses made sure she slept and wasn't bothered. The nurses took care of the twins while Lisa rested.

The next day, Lisa woke up to a room full of balloons, flowers and smiling faces. Everyone was there, well almost everyone, accept Eugene. As she thought about Eugene she became sad because she wished he were there to witness the birth of their children. Lisa was able to leave the hospital that same day with the twin boys. Mrs. Wilson took Lisa home. Mrs. Wilson had the room set up for Lisa and the twins.

On December 12, Eugene and his attorney, Mr. Zokeski, entered the courtroom. Mr. Zokeski talked to Eugene prior to court starting. Eugene asked Mr. Zokeski, "What do you think about his case?"

Mr. Zokeski replied, "I am going to ask for a motion for you to stay in juvenile court and that your case remains separate from your co-defendant."

Eugene said, "Okay."

Everyone was in the courtroom that day. Eugene only got a glimpse of Lisa holding the twins because the bailiff wouldn't let him look too long. But he was excited about the babies. His lawyer, Mr. Zokeski, gave him the news of the babies being born. Eugene had been locked in the box and he couldn't use the phone, so he did not find out about the birth of his babies until Mr. Zokeski told him.

The judge entered the courtroom and the bailiff announced that court was now in session. Mr. Zokeski introduced himself to the court and informed the court that he was representing Eugene Gardner. They proceeded in court. Mr. Zokeski filed a motion so that Eugene could stay in juvenile court and be tried separate from his co-defendant, Locsta. The motion was granted. The D.A. didn't object. The judge asked the D.A. and Mr. Zokeski if they were ready to proceed to trial and to set a trial date.

Mr. Zokeski was pushing for a speedy trial because he felt confident about winning this case because of lack of evidence against Eugene. The evidence against Eugene was hearsay, such as, a girl who said that she recognized Eugene's voice. They had no murder weapon nor did they have any witnesses that could identify Eugene as the shooter. The judge granted the speedy trial and set the trial date for January 16. Court was adjourned, but not before Eugene's lawyer asked the judge if he could stipulate an order in place where Eugene could see his girlfriend and twin babies while in juvenile hall. The judge granted the request and said he would grant the order.

Locsta...

Donald (Locsta) was in the Criminal Court Building also being charged with murder, because his car was used in commission of a crime. His lawyer told him that he could possibly get the charges dropped but the D.A. wanted Donald to turn state's evidence and give up the shooter. Locsta said, "I am no snitch."

Locsta's lawyer asked, "Are you willing to take a plea?"

Locsta asked, "What type of deal are you offering?"

"Well, I might be able to get you ten years."

"Ten years, damn! I got to think about that."

"Okay, I'm going to talk to the D.A and see what he says because I don't think he wants to take this case to trial. So I'm going to ask for a continuance for about a month. You need to think about this and have your mind made by then. Is that good for you?

Locsta is now a little confused, he replied, "Yeah, okay."

Locsta's attorney asked the court for a continuance. The judge asked Locsta if he agreed to the continuance. Locsta said, "Yes." The continuance was granted. The judge scheduled the next court date for January 14.

Lisa visits Eugene

Lisa entered Los Padrinos Juvenile Hall with the twins. The twins were now two weeks old and they were getting bigger. This was going to be the first time that Eugene was going to have physical contact with Lisa and their children. Lisa waited for about five minutes before Eugene came out. When she saw him, she could barely contain herself. She was happy and sad at the same time. They kissed and hugged. Eugene was excited about holding his babies for the first time. The twins cried for a little bit, but after a while they calmed down. Eugene just kept telling the twins, "It's me, Daddy." The visit lasted an hour. Eugene talked with Lisa about their future and played with the twins. Eugene told Lisa that they were going to get married and be a family once he got out of there. When the visit was over, Eugene had to go back to his unit. He kissed Lisa and the twins good-bye and told them that he loved them. It was hard for Eugene and Lisa to say goodbye, but they got through it. The next time they would be seeing each other would be in court on January 16.

January 12th ...

Locsta was in his cell when the deputy called his name. "Donald Smith, you have a visit."

Locsta exited his cell and walked to the deputy who then gave Locsta his visiting pass and told him he had an attorney visit. Locsta walked to the area where the attorney visits were held. He was seated in front of his attorney, Mr. Sullivan.

"How are you Donald?"

"Man, I'm okay. Getting tired of this shit, but it is what it is."

"Well, I can understand. I got good news for you. I talked to the District Attorney and he's willing to drop the murder charges to accessory to a murder and offer you ten years with eighty percent."

"Well, I been thinking and I will take the deal."

Mr. Sullivan was really surprised. He said, "Okay. We will be back in court in two days and everything will be ready."

"Okay and thank you."

"You're welcome. I will see you in court.

Locsta's court date, January 14th...

Locsta entered the courtroom and sat next to his lawyer. They made small talk because they know what was going to happen today. The judge entered the courtroom and sat on the bench.

The judge stated, "The charges have been dismissed and the defendant is entering a plea of guilty to accessory to murder, correct?"

Mr. Sullivan and the D.A. both said, "Yes."

The judge asked, "Donald Smith, how do you plead to these charges?"

"Guilty, your honor."

Judge stated, "The defendant has entered a plea of guilty and is sentenced to ten years in State Prison. Court is adjourned and Locsta is escorted back to his holding cell. He will go back to the Los Angeles County Jail where he will be there until he goes to State Prison."

Eugene's court date, January 16th...

It's the start of the speedy trial and detective Taylor is on the stand. The D.A. asked him some questions about himself, like his name and how long he's been on the force.

Detective Taylor replied, "My name is David J. Taylor and I have been on the police force for seventeen years."

The D.A then said, "Tell the court what happened when Teresa Jenkins came to the police station and spoke to you?"

"Well, Ms. Jenkins and two friends came into the station and told the officer at the front desk that she had some information pertaining to a murder that took place."

"Who murdered?"

"It was Clarence Jones aka Squeak and Arnold aka Lil' Scrooge."

"So were these two involved in a gang?"

"Yes, they both were members of a street gang called G.M."

"Okay, now back to when Ms. Jenkins said she had information to the murders, how did she obtain this information?"

"She was there when it took place."

D.A. for clearer understanding, he asked, "When you say she was there, where exactly was she?"

"She was in the car with the now deceased when it happened."

"What was the information she gave you?"

"Ms. Jenkins gave me a license plate number that came back to a Donald Smith."

Attorney Zokeski jumped up. "Objection, your honor. That individual has no relevance to this case."

Judge said, "Sustained. D.A., please stick to the relevance of this case."

"Yes." D.A then asked, "Well, detective Taylor, what else did she tell you?"

"Ms. Jenkins also told me that one of the perps yelled out 'What's up now?' and that she recognized the voice."

"So she was able to give you a description by hearing a voice?"

"Yes."

"Who did she describe?"

"She described the defendant, Eugene Gardner."

"Thank you. I have no further questions, your honor."

The Lonely Child

Judge asked, "Mr. Zokeski, do you care to cross-examine?"

"Yes, your honor." He turned to Detective Taylor and said, "You know that you are under oath, right?"

"Yes."

"When Ms. Jenkins told you she recognized the voice of the defendant, was she able to describe him or point him out in a photo lineup?"

"No."

"Matter of fact has Ms. Jenkins ever laid eyes on the defendant?"

"No."

"Now, detective, is it possible from your experience in the field or in the line of duty to witness a homicide that people can become hysterical and go into somewhat of a post dramatic syndrome temporarily?"

Detective Taylor, in his mind trying to figure out where the attorney was going with this question, replied, "Yes, it is possible."

"Is it also possible that his is the case with Ms. Jenkins?"

Detective Taylor paused for a moment then said, "Well, um, I don't know."

"How long was it after the murder took place that Ms. Jenkins decided to come forward?"

"It was approximately four months after the murders took place."

"Can we assume that by the length of time she decided to come forward that maybe someone told her to say what she said?"

Detective Taylor, feeling a little nervous, he is now perspiring profusely. "Yes, it is possible."

"No further questions."

D.A. said, "Excuse me, your honor, may I approach the bench?"

"Yes, Counsel, please approach."

D.A. remarked, "I will not be using Ms. Jenkins' testimony so it's grounds for a dismissal."

Judge turns to Mr. Zokeski for his reaction to the D.A.'s comment?

Mr. Zokeski said, "I agree, your honor. I didn't think this case would make it this far."

Judge replied, "Yes, this is a waste of taxpayer's money and a waste of our time. The case will be dismissed. Please step back." Judge turned to Mr. Gardner and said, "Today is your lucky day, Mr. Gardner, because the charges against you are being dismissed."

Eugene just smiled and hugged his attorney. The courtroom went crazy with excitement.

Judge said, "Order in the court," as she pounded his gavel. After the court calmed down, the judge said, "Mr. Gardner, you are free to go."

Eugene was released from court and his whole family was in the courtroom waiting on him. Eugene got hugs and kisses from his family and friends. He grabbed Lisa and kissed her long and hard and asked her to marry him. Lisa said yes.

June 23rd...

Eugene's and Lisa's wedding was held at the Los Angeles Christian Center. The wedding was big with all of their family and friends in attendance. Well all of Lisa's friends because Eugene's friends were dead or in jail. It was the wedding of the year! Eugene and Lisa said their vows and the pastor married them.

Eugene was a family man now. He's taking responsibility for his wife and kids. Eugene wrote Locsta and some other homies as often as possible. They all were happy for him and encouraged Eugene to stay positive.

CPSIA information can be obtained
at www.ICGtesting.com
Printed in the USA
BVHW040209100323
659973BV00004B/540

9 780615 746296